PLUG ENT. AND ONESTOP ENT.

Tommy White & Brooklyn Brown

THE PLUG'S COUNSEL

BOOK 3

INSPIRED BY **GHETTO THE PLUG**
WRITTEN BY **HANCHO**

Tommy White and Brooklyn Brown

THE PLUG'S COUNCEL

BOOK 3

Inspired By
GHETTO THE PLUG
Written By **HANCHO**

Cover Designed by Dynastys' Visionary Designs
www.facebook.com/dynastys.coverme

EDITED BY: Dynastys' Visionary Designs

Google Ghetto The Plug on all social networks.
If you need your book published contact me at 678-516-5997

PLUG ENTERTAINMENT
https://tinyurl.com/ghettotheplug

CHECK OUT MUSIC BY GHETTO THE PLUG

ALSO SEARCH AND BUY MY MUSIC ON HTTPS://TINYURL.COM/GHETTOTHEPLUG

IT'S WORTH THE BUY!

ABOUT THE AUTHOR

My name is GOOGLE friendly. Look me up! I have done a lot in the music industry. You have to get your music on sites like iTunes or cdbaby for people to buy. It takes a lot of grinding, going state to state chasing the dream, and never giving up.

You can also write me. Just call this number for information (330-388-3663), and we can go from there. Thanks for listening!

I'm going to leave you with this. Don't chase the money, chase the dream and the money will come. Stay focused. When I say I'm the plug, trust me. I am everything that has to do with music. I can find or put you in the right places. Get with me!

Check out all my books on amazon.com by searching GHETTO THE PLUG. I do it all!

Hook:
Ferrari, mozerati, bently, rafe
Ferrari, mozerati, bently, rafe
Ferrari, mozerati, bently, rafe
I got a bag now might cop all them joints today

This is just a sample of a hook I threw together off the top. If you're interested, get with me. I got plenty of tracks and all are for sale on my cdbaby site. On the next page I have information for sale for artist who want to become a rapper.

ACKNOWLEDGMENTS

First, I'd like to than Allah. I'd also like to thank Ghetto for giving me a chance to write a book inspired by him. Also, I'd like to thank Nathan Welch aka Fat Nate from Washington D.C. for letting me know that I could write and motivating me to continue to write my first book. I want to thank both my parents for supporting and loving me during my hard times.

Shout out to all the good men that I met during my journey in the Federal and State system. Shout out LO (VA), Manni (VA) Spanish Manny (NY), 40 (NY), Pooh (VA), Jim Bob (OH), Fatz (Detroit), Blickem (DC), WhiteBoy (DC), KC (VA), Biscuit (VA), JPooh (VA), Mean (VA), Bounta (OH), Kill Will (OH), glad ya'll two made it home and those I forgot to shout out. I didn't forget about ya'll. Just know we'll all make it home one day. Inshallah.

Chapter 1

Akron, Ohio lay calmly under thick grey increasing clouds that promised a severe thunderstorm in the making. The skyline was a mixture of dark and light clouds. The darkest clouds hovered over the small section where all the trailers gathered to form a little community. In this community, there were a total of forty-three trailers all side by side. The grocery store, local bar, and local clubs. It was within walking distance of the only elementary school in the town. The location was in a perfect spot. For most trailer park owners, being this close to everything made living there convenient.

For this reason, Kevin White brought his family to this area. He decided this slightly after his wife, Debby White got sick. However, with this change of venue came a change in his attitude. Stress, depression, frustration, empty promises, and helplessness consumed Kevin. His desperate urge to find someone who could cure his wife turned him into a biter man. A man who never considered turning to God with a prayer request to heal his wife. His wife's illness created a monster out of him. He became a man who no longer knew any boundaries of respect.

Since his wife was diagnosed with an irreversible disease, liquor became his companion. What started as just casual drinks to ease his stress, quickly turned into an excessive bad habit. It turned a hard-working, good husband, and father into someone easily hated. His compulsive drinking disorder made him a nasty man. The liquor turned him into someone not even his family recognized. Most of the family stayed away from him intentionally. Although they were highly concerned about Debby, they wanted no ties to Kevin any longer. The family disowned him until he stopped drinking.

So, as long as the bottle remained his friend, his family refused to acknowledge his existence. The last time he spoke to anyone in his family was during the Christmas holidays. This was approximately sixteen months ago, and nothing changed since. This caused him to move out of his place and bring his small family to a trailer house complex.

"Can I go watch television?" Tommy asked his father while walking to the small living room section of the trailer.

"What do you want to watch?" Kevin asked angrily while drinking Smirnoff Vodka straight with no chase.

"I want to see basketball," Tommy said, pretending he had a basketball in his hand, taking a fade-away jump shot.

"Who's playing?" Kevin asked, taking a sip from the bottle.

"Labron James," Tommy said excitedly.

"You and this damn Labron James. That's all you seem to know," Kevin said, with specks of saliva flying out of his mouth.

"When I get older, I want to be just like Labron James. He's the best player in the League. No one can see King James," Tommy said smiling.

"What? You don't want to be like your daddy?" Kevin asked feeling insulted, then took a big gulp of his vodka.

"I want to be like Lebron!" Tommy said aggressively.

He looked at his father confused. All Tommy ever knew was bad breath, alcohol, and abusive words from his dad. Even at his young age, he knew his father was no good.

"You don't even know how to play!" Kevin teased his son. Kevin felt that chasing dreams were for abusive drunks who talked nasty all day.

"I know how to play," Tommy protested.

"Who taught you?" Kevin challenged sarcastically.

"My friends," Tommy said, thinking about Bobby who lived a few trailers down to the left.

"What friends?" Kevin asked, adjusting his body inside the recliner. Shifting his body to face his son. He warned himself not to slap blood out of Tommy's mouth if he started talking about his imaginary lawyer friend.

"My friend Bobby."

"Who's Bobby?"

"He lives a few houses down. I play basketball with him all the time." Tommy said. He knew his father was about to sock him if he mentioned his imaginary friend.

"Is he any good?" Kevin asked, leaning backwards in the recliner. He settled down after his son spoke without referring to someone who didn't exist.

"I'll let you watch television after you check on your mother. See if she needs anything," Kevin slurred.

"So, I can watch Lebron after I check on mommy?" Tommy questioned again for clarity.

"Go check on your mother, then you can watch television." Kevin waved his son off.

Tommy hustled down the small hallway and pushed open his mother's bedroom door. He watched her look up, and over her shoulder to see who was coming into the room. Tommy rushed over to her smiling.

"Hey, mom!" Tommy said energetically.

"Yes baby," Debby said with a weak voice.

She turned her pale face to look at her son. Her small petite frame looked like she was one step away from looking like a skeleton, and the skin on her face was sunken around her eyes.

Debby was one of the most beautiful women who lived in Ohio state. In her early years, she was labeled and crowned, Ms. Ohio. That moment changed her life. She had a bright future until she was attacked by some virus that eats away at cell molecules. The family doctor did little to stabilize her. She'd gone to several other doctors in Ohio, but none were equipped with the knowledge to treat her condition. So, due to her not having proper treatment, her condition worsened day by day. What kept her strong was the fact that her son still needed her.

"Yes, baby," she replied.

"Do you need anything?" Tommy asked, giving his mother a hug and kiss.

He didn't know what was wrong with his mother, but he know she wasn't the same. He knew she was sick and weak.

"Why? What's going on?" Debby was concerned.

"Dad told me to check on you. Are you alright?" Tommy noticed his mother barely had the strength to hug him back.

"Can you get me a glass of water?" Debby asked with a slight smile.

"Sure, mom. Is that all you need?" Tommy inquired before leaving the room.

"For now. Can you make it warm? I have to take my medication," Debby's voice cracked as she instructed.

"Alright, mommy. I'll be right back."

With the cup in his mouth, he climbed down careful not to fall. He opened the sink cabinet, pulled out a bottle of water since it was luke warm already, and poured it into the cup. Once he was done, he rushed back to his mother.

"Here's your cup of water, mommy," Tommy said politely.

"Thank you very much, baby," Debby said struggling to sit up in bed. She grabbed her plate on the nightstand that had all her medication on it.

"Are you feeling better?" Tommy asked, watching her take her medication.

"I'm feeling much better," Debby lied. She could never tell her baby boy what was wrong or how she truly felt.

"You should be all better soon," Tommy encouraged.

"Why?" she asked looking at her son.

"My friend's mother was sick. She's all better now. So, you should be too," Tommy concluded, hoping this was truly the case.

"What friend is this?" Debby wasn't sure who he was referring to as a friend. For a second, she thought he was going to say his imaginary lawyer friend.

"My friend, Bobby from a few houses down," Tommy replied and pointed at the bedroom walls as if she could see through them.

The Kindlemare family has a son named Bobby, and they lived a few houses down.

"Alright, baby, I should be better soon too," Debby lied again. "You don't have to worry about me. I'm going to be fine."

"Can I go watch basketball now?" Tommy asked, thinking about Lebron James slamming the basketball on a bunch of guys who couldn't stop him.

"Sure, son. Go ahead."

Tommy ran out of the bedroom to watch television. He turned it on and switched to ESPN where Lebron was playing. The moment it came on, Lebron was slam-dunking the basketball in the face of two opposing players. This is why Tommy loved to watch Lebron show out.

Chapter 2

Kevin heard the sound of his son playing with his XBOX system he brought him for his birthday. The sound of a crowd screaming because of a special dunk by Lebron James made him look at the bedroom wall that connected both bedrooms.

"That boy loves that game," Kevin said calmly.

"He loves Lebron James. Our son is a basketball freak," Debby said smiling.

"I just hope that game doesn't taint his brain," Kevin said seriously.

"What's going on with you? You seem to be in a really bad mood, again," Debby said, using all her strength to turn and face her husband in bed.

"I'm just thinking," Kevin plainly stated.

"Thinking about what?"

Debby was now concerned. She prayed this conversation with the love of her life didn't turn into one of his nasty, violating dirty talks. Her heart didn't have the strength to keep enduring the verbal abuse his mouth cooked up. His mouth turned so dirty when she got sick, he wasn't the same man she married.

"I don't like this little fake community," Kevin admitted, instantly looking out of the window. The loud noise coming from the next door neighbor was disturbing. "I thought this would be a good opportunity to finally be still until I could find a doctor to make things right. Guess I was wrong."

"I don't see anything wrong," Debby said softly.

"You don't see shit! You're always in bed. How the fuck can you see?" Kevin roared.

"I'm in bed because I'm sick," Debby replied.

"I know, I know. Woman, I know all about it. I have to deal with it every day too!" Kevin said aggressively.

"You're not physically going through it. I'm the one suffering. I'm the one hurting every day," Debby said with pressure building up in her chest.

"What? You must be out of your mind! I'm suffering too! Shit, I'm probably suffering more than you!" Kevin yelled, pointing angrily in Debby's direction.

Kevin sat up in the bed and snatched the bed spread backwards, tossing it near Debby's face. He got out of bed, grabbed his boxers, and put them back on. He then reached for his favorite t-shirt that read, *'I'm an Alcoholic! Who gives a shit!'* He looked at his wife, deciding he needed a strong drink to ease his nerves.

"We're fixing to move," Kevin mumbled, walking down the hallway, and into the kitchen opening the cabinet with a child-proof lock on it.

"When?" Debby asked.

"Soon."

Kevin almost jumped out of his skin when he realized Debbie got out of bed and walked to the kitchen behind him.

"Where to?"

Debbie wondered, assuming it was across town where the other trailer section was.

"Not sure," Kevin replied honestly.

"So, do you have a plan?" Debby was confused. "This seems to be a spare of the moment decision."

"I got one," Kevin said, thinking about the world's famous Twin Towers and Empire State building.

"What is it?" she asked dryly.

"I'm going to move us to New York," he announced, then waited to see her reaction.

"Why New York?" she asked calmly, trying to figure out why not Los Angeles, or Florida.

"That's where you always wanted to go." He smiled like he did the best thing in the world for her.

"Not since I've been sick," she admitted seriously. "Everything has changed."

"Hold on. I have to go get a bottle for this."

"You need to stop drinking," Debby tried to convince her husband once again that he has a real problem.

"Don't worry about what the fuck I'm doing!" Kevin snapped, caring less about his wife's feelings. He couldn't stand being nagged about his liquor.

"Stop cursing at me," Debby said with a strong cough.

"Who the fuck you think you are? You's a dirty bitch! You deserve everything you got coming to you," Kevin shouted. He launched at her like he was about to slap her.

"Your mouth is so foul." She hated when he got like this.

"Do something about it!" Kevin drew closer to her personal space, looking down at her in disgust. "You're not going to do shit!"

"You're so damn mean." Debby started to cry.

"We're moving because of you," Kevin said honestly. "It's my soul reason for wanting better."

"What do you mean because of me?" Debby inquired, feeling like less of a woman. She thought for a second that he was going to cast blame.

"I need to find you a better doctor," Kevin said sadly.

"You believe New York will help?" Debby asked calmly.

"Some of the most respected doctors come out of New York. We need to get away from this Akron place. Aren't you tired of living out of a trailer?" Kevin asked angrily.

He couldn't stand living in Ohio, especially Akron city. It's a pure hell hole.

"You know I hate it," Debby tried to convince him.

"Alright, we moving to New York to find a good doctor. Plus, you'll finally get to see the Big Apple drop on New Year's Eve. We always talked about that. Now it's your big chance." Kevin assumed this is what she always wanted.

"Did you tell Tommy yet?" she asked sincerely and politely.

"No. I'll let him know in a little while." Kevin took a deep breath.

"How do you think he's going to feel about moving again?"

"Who the hell cares? He's a child. He don't get no damn say-so in nothing! He'll love New York. The schools there are better than this Akron place."

He couldn't believe she actually asked him how Tommy would feel about moving like he had a say in the matter. She didn't even have a say in the matter. It wasn't up for debate. Kevin made up his mind already and decided on what section he'll be moving them to.

"This move will affect him too, he should have a say too," Debbie tried to defend her only son.

"He's only ten fucking years old!" Kevin yelled. "Ain't no damn ten-year-old going to dictate nothing."

"But he'll have to switch schools again," she said sadly knowing that Tommy hated switching schools.

"Who gives a damn." Kevin grabbed his liquor bottle, further losing his sense of reasoning. "We're not moving for our son; we're moving for you!" Kevin said aggressively, shaking his head. "I'm putting your needs above all. I need you to get better."

"Whatever you say," Debby rolled her eyes and laid back down in bed.

"It's always what the fuck I say," Kevin challenged. He could never please her or make her happy. The illness took over their sex life, so he had no release. Just pent-up frustration that caused him to step out on his wife a few times.

"Your right, babe. It's time for me to take my medication. Can you bring me a glass of Pepsi?" she said quickly before he exploded with disrespect.

"Pepsi? You're supposed to drink water," he replied while storming out of the bedroom to oblige his wife's request. While in there, he looked at his son watching another basketball game. He heard the referee scream foul on Lebron James. He shook his head, knowing his son was completely hooked on the King. Reaching inside the cabinet he found a clean cup and removed one of the water bottles from another cabinet. Holding it up to the light, he realized there were little fizz bubbles, and changed the bottle because he grabbed seltzer water by accident.

After fixing her water, he carried it back inside the bedroom. Stepping inside he watched her pour different pills into her trembling hand. Although he loved her dearly, he desperately wanted to strangle her. He hated that she allowed that virus to kick her ass.

"Here's your damn water," Kevin said rudely, holding the cup in her face until she was ready to take it.

"Thank you, honey," Debby said sarcastically.

She knew her illness was taking a huge toll on her family. She figured a new environment could be helpful. Especially, if it will put her in a more suitable position for the medical treatment she needed to kick the virus bug and restore her health.

"What the fuck ever, man. You're fucking welcome. Now hurry the hell up and take your medication. Dumb ass cunt," Kevin snapped viciously.

"Why do you keep talking to me like that?" Debby asked, fighting back tears. She didn't know what was worst; his foul tongue or the damn virus tearing down her life support.

"Take your fucking medication already. Shut your damn pie hole, and handle your business," Kevin exploded again out of frustration.

He walked out of the bedroom, went into the living room, and stood in front of the television. Looking down at his son, he could see his wife's features all in his face. The only thing Tommy had that resembled his father was his nose and ears. Everything else was Debby's.

"We're moving," Kevin revealed calmly, taking a long swig from his liquor bottle. "You got something to say about that son?" Kevin looked down intimidatingly.

"Where to Dad?" Tommy asked hyped up. He hated this area. He was craving for new scenery.

"You're not mad?" Kevin examined his son intently, surprised that he hadn't started whining like a little girl.

"No. I've been wanting to move. I don't like the people here. There're hardly any kids around here for me to play with," Tommy said honestly.

"You're not going to miss your friends?" Kevin asked with a slurred speech. The liquor was taking hold of his consciousness.

"No!" Tommy said frowning his face.

"Why not?" Kevin was confused.

"I have no real friends, dad," Tommy said honestly.

"That's perfect. We're moving to the big city. New York City. The Big Apple, the city that never sleeps," Kevin slurred again.

"Anywhere is better than here, Dad. When are we leaving?" Tommy was ready to go.

"I didn't tell your mother, but we're out of here first thing in the morning," Kevin whispered when he told Tommy.

He rubbed his son's head and walked back into the bedroom. Once inside, he collapsed onto the bed beside Debby and started snoring.

Chapter 3

Kevin waited patiently in the waiting room for any word about his wife and her health. It was now close to three o'clock in the afternoon, and the doctor was just coming out of the main room.

"What's going on with my wife?" Kevin asked the doctor surrounded by a group of nurses.

"She's been diagnosed with stage three ovarian cancer," Doctor Alvin sympathetically stated.

"What can you do for her?" Kevin desperately needed to know.

"We're going to run a few tests. The cancer has spread tremendously throughout her body, even to her lungs now," Dr. Alvin said softly.

"What does that mean?" Kevin was devastated.

"It means your situation is irreversible," Dr. Alvin stated truthfully.

"What about chemo therapy, or that new laser stuff that zaps cancer cells away?" Kevin asked desperately.

"Your wife is too far along," Dr. Alvin said placing his hands on Kevin's shoulders.

"And?" Kevin said suspiciously hoping and praying he could do something.

"There's nothing we can do here. Had you come during her early stages, we might have had a better chance to help her. This type of cancer is extremely aggressive. It spreads fast once it reaches critical stages."

"So, what are you going to do now?"

He turned around looking at all the people dressed in rags and garbs. His eyes connected with a few sympathetic nurses who bowed their heads in respect.

"We're going to keep her here for another week. We're going to run more tests and search for an answer. However, we believe she doesn't have much longer," Dr. Alvin repeated.

"What are you saying?" Kevin scratched his head, refusing to accept Dr. Alvin's prognosis.

"I'm saying you and your family should cherish her remaining time together. We predict a six-month omen," Dr. Alvin suggested.

"What the hell is that?" Kevin snapped. "That can't be right doctor. Are you sure about this? There has to be a mistake."

"She only has six months to live," Alvin repeated a third time, hoping his words resonated in Kevin's mind this time.

"Listen, Doctor, we came here because we were led to believe this place here in New York has top-notch cancer experts. The best doctors, and the best resources. Now you're telling me my wife won't be here in six months?" Kevin lost it, unable to stop the stray tears from rolling down his face.

"I'm sorry, Mr. White. This is all I can tell you. You came here when your wife was at stage two, and the cancer quickly progressed to stage three. Cancer is best treated before stage two," Doctor Alvin Showmiyer said while looking at Debby's chart. He scanned down the list of tests that were already taken. He reviewed the keynotes from his nurses.

"Alright, man listen. How much will surgery cost me to have the cancer cells cut out?" Kevin asked humbly.

He knew that in New York money talks. Having money could change the outcome of most situations. However, this wasn't that kind of situation.

"That type of surgery should, and can only be done during the early stages, not at stage three. I'm sorry," the doctor said trying to ignore the man's proposal for more money.

Alvin knew money wasn't the issue here. The problem is they waited too long to get treatment.

"What's the point of running more test then?" Kevin pried, as his heart broke, and beat erratically in his chest.

"We need to see if we missed anything, we need to find out if her blood reacts to certain medication, and to make one hundred and ten percent sure that there's nothing else we can do," Alvin insisted calmly. He knew this was a delicate situation.

"Give me her full medical report. I want to go online, and search other countries for a possible specialist who can turn this around," Kevin requested respectfully.

"I've searched already. But, if it relaxes your nerves, I'll provide you with a full report. My nurse will have it for you in a few minutes." He nodded his head to his assistant nurse.

"I'm doing the very best I can and I will continue to do so even if I can't find something to prolong her life. I will do what I can to ensure your wife's comfort. I suggest you go home and get some rest and come back tomorrow."

****

Tommy sat in class all day daydreaming. He imagined himself being filthy rich, having enough money to bring his mother's health back to normal. He knew his family needed money badly. When he was a little younger, he didn't understand his situation and assumed things were how they were supposed to be. But, now that he's hit high school and thinking about college, he knew that he had to maintain above-average grades.

Tommy thought about how he'd respond to his mother when he got home. She was due to be released today. At least, that's what he was told. He prayed she made it through this horrible fight for her life. His thoughts were interrupted by the three o'clock bell. He stood up and walked behind the rest of his classmates. They were in line one by one picking up their report cards. Tommy opened his while walking down the hallway. He smiled at the straight roll of A's. Every year, each report card was filled with A's and B's. This was the best one yet. All his hard work and studying had paid off.

"Hey, Tommy. What did you get this time?" A girl name Amanda asked him, trying to peak over his shoulders.

Amanda was a fair skin girl who wore bifocal glasses and braces. She was one of the girls who noticed Tommy was a smart kid.

"I got straight A's this time," Tommy said, holding up his report card.

"That's great! You keep that up for the next several years, and you're going to have colleges fighting to get you. You still want to be a lawyer?" Amanda asked, walking side-by-side with him in the hallway.

"I know I can't wait to get home to show my mother," Tommy smiled. "This will make her feel much better."

"How is she?" Amanda asked sadly.

"I'll know when she comes home."

"She still in the hospital?"

"Pretty much."

"I pray she gets well soon. I'll see you tomorrow."

Tommy knew she was just being nosy. He put his report card away and headed straight uptown to his house. He rode the four-express train to 125th street, then walked the rest of the way. When he arrived home, he expected his mother's presence. However, she was nowhere to be found.

He opened his parent's bedroom door and his father was lying across the bed crying.

"Hey, Dad, what's up?"

"Shut the fuck up, and close my damn door," Kevin screamed with drunken slurred speech.

"Where's mom?" Tommy asked not budging from the doorway.

"Motherfucker, didn't I say to close my damn door. Your mother is in the hospital," Kevin cursed.

"I thought today was her release day?" Tommy asked ignoring his father's attitude from being drunk.

"There keeping her for more fucking test. The doctor said she ain't got nothing but a six-month life span left," Kevin said reaching for the liquor bottle that had spilled all over the floor.

Tommy rushed inside the room. He kicked the liquor bottle. It slammed against the back wall.

"What did you just say?"

"Your mother may only have six months left to live. The cancer spread every motherfucking where in her body," Kevin cried heavily, curling up in a fetal position, and sobbed. "We're going to fucking lose her boy," Kevin exploded.

****

Several months later, Debby passed away. They held a small service for her and later held one for her friends and other family members. Family came in from all over the world to pay their respect to Debby. From the moment they buried Debby, Kevin had completely changed for the worse. He started verbally abusing Tommy. They were in debt, and could barely afford a coven stone for the grave. This created tension between Kevin and Tommy. Tommy knew they had money problems, and it was now mandatory that he got good grades. He needed to finish school and become the best lawyer he could be.

Chapter 4

Since Tommy has been going to school in Harlem, he's been running into some problems with a few bullies from around the way. They love to harass other kids when they were alone. Usually, they harassed kids for pocket change and lunch money. Recently, they were just plain old bullying people because they could. Most of the kids they picked on were a lot smaller than them. Fat Billy is one of the neighborhood's top bullies. A big young kid who hung with older kids. Since he was the youngest, he had to work harder to show the older kids he could hold his own. This was normal while his older buddies were around. He had to poke his chest out and stand tall. When the other kids weren't around Fat Billy was still tough, but he could be dealt with.

For years, Fat Billy earned a reputation in the Harlem area. His reputation came with a misguided confidence in himself. So, he regularly searched the streets, and schools for new prey. Lately, Tommy has been his focus. It just so happened that Tommy was walking down the street by himself. He ran up behind Tommy, shoved him to the ground, and started laughing.

"What's your problem?" Tommy asked, looking up at Fat Billy.

"You're my problem," Fat Billy said smirking.

He found it funny when people talked crap to him from the ground. Especially when he's the reason they were down there in the first place.

"Where's my money?"

"I don't owe you no money," Tommy said, trying to get back on his feet.

"As long as you're alive you owe me," Fat Billy said.

"Dude! Leave me alone," Tommy said, not intimidated.

"Hey, Fat Billy!" Chance screamed at the top of his lungs. He was walking up fast behind Fat Billy.

"What?" Fat Billy shouted turning around noticing Lil Woo, Chance, Scooter, and Ryder walking in his direction.

"Leave him alone before we kick your ass the way it needs to be kicked," Lil' Woo threatened, stepping up to approach Fat Billy. "That's our boy."

Fat Billy Looked around realizing that he was outnumbered. "Alright, I'll leave him alone. I didn't know he had any friends," Fat Billy said walking away.

"Thanks a lot, guys. My name is Tommy," he said looking at everyone. He tried not to, but his eyes kept going back and forth from the boys to the girl hanging with them. Tommy couldn't believe how beautiful the girl in the little group was. He fell in love with her at first sight. It was like something you only witnessed in movies or on television.

"My name is Lil' Woo. This here is Chance," Lil' Woo said pointing him out.

"What's up. Please to meet you," Chance said, nodding his head respectfully.

"This is Scooter," Lil' Woo introduced, pointing in his direction.

"What's popping?" Scooter said, extending his arm to embrace a hand shake.

"And, this is the beautiful, Ryder." Lil' Woo smiled.

"How are you? Are you alright? Did they hurt you?" Ryder asked, looking Tommy up and down. She checked for signs of injuries. They weren't sure how long Fat Billy and his posse had Tommy hemmed up.

"I'm fine, thanks to you guys they didn't hurt me. They tried to ruff me up a bit, but I'm cool," Tommy said honestly, unable to peel his eyes away from Ryder. His strong stares caused her to blush.

"What was that all about?" Lil' Woo questioned.

"Just bullying. That big one doesn't have nothing else to do but mess with people," Tommy divulged.

"That's Fat Billy. He likes to throw his weight around," Chance interjected.

"Someone needs to kick his ass, for real," Scooter said seriously.

"Where you from?" Chance asked while listening to Tommy's accent.

"I'm from Akron, Ohio," Tommy said while cutting his eyes from Chance to Ryder.

"I've seen you around for a while. How long have you lived out here in Harlem?" Lil Woo questioned, wanting to know what the deal was with the white boy who couldn't stop eyeing Ryder.

"For a little over a year now," Tommy replied.

"Why did you leave Ohio?" Scooter asked.

"I moved here with my parents. My mother was sick, and my father believed that New York had the best doctors and resources in the country," Tommy said sadly.

"I don't know about the country, but Mount Sinai Hospital does have some top-notch doctors there. The technology is outrageously awesome. So, your dad made the right decision," Lil Woo told him.

"Do you have any friends around here?" Ryder asked.

"No, I don't. I mostly stay to myself. I'm a real school junky. I normally don't have time to make new friends," Tommy told her truthfully.

"You can be friends with us," Ryder offered, waving her hands in front of everyone.

"Yeah, you can be our new homie," Scooter confirmed, figuring a new member of the crew wouldn't hurt.

"What school do you go to?" Lil' Woo asked, wondering if he's attending school in Harlem, in the Bronx, Brooklyn, or Queens.

I'm in junior high school forty-three. It's located on 129th street on Amsterdam Avenue," Tommy said assuming that they never heard of the place.

"We know where that is. Shit, we all go to the same school," Chance said excitedly.

"Damn, things must be hard on you and your family. I hope your mother gets better," Scooter said. "I just lost my mother to breast cancer."

"My mother had ovarian cancer," Tommy said sadly. "She didn't make it."

"That's one of the most vicious cancers you can have. I read about all the different kinds of cancers," Scooter said shaking his head.

"We're going to say a prayer for our new homie's mother tonight at eight o'clock sharp. We all should pray no matter what's going on for Tommy's mother," Chance said slapping Tommy on the shoulder.

"Praying to God does work. You just need to be sincere about your prayers. Mean each word from the heart. God can, and will heal," Scooter said seriously.

"Make sure you let everyone know that your Lil' Woo's homie. That way, no one will mess with you no more. You don't need extra stress with your mother being sick and all," Chance said.

"One more thing, we walk to and from school together," Lil' Woo said.

"That's right. We meet on 125th Street in the morning. After school, we meet in front of the school. No one leaves until the whole crew is accounted for," Chance said getting hyped.

"That's correct. We move as a unit. We pretty much do everything together. You'll see," Lil' Woo assured.

"Is this some kind of gang?" Tommy asked while soaking everything in. He concluded that they were a gang, but he wasn't the one to sit back and assume.

"Negative, Batman," Scooter joked. "I don't deal with gangs or gang members. That gang stuff is whack. I can hold my own. I've knocked out grown-ass men before. I hit hard."

"My name isn't Batman," Tommy said. He was offended that they referred to him as a man dressed up in black spandex tights.

"That's a figure of speech. I didn't call you Batman," Scooter said laughing.

"My bad," Tommy blew out a breath he didn't realize he was holding. He felt silly.

"It's cool. You're alright," Ryder encouraged, placing her hands on Tommy's shoulder. "You're with us now."

Chapter 5

Tommy woke up feeling energetic. He rushed to the shower and took care of his hygiene. Afterward, he got dressed and search his clothes from the other day for Ryder's number. He was so panicky his blood pressure rose because he couldn't find it. All night he thought about what he'd say to her. He was so crazy about her, that he didn't want to mess anything up by saying something foolish. He destroyed his room looking for the small piece of paper Ryder wrote her number on. He made so much noise his father came out of the room enraged.

"Tommy!" his father yelled.

"Yes!" Tommy replied.

"The fuck your dumb ass doing? Do you want me to fuck you up? You must be trying to get your ass kicked with all that noise?" Kevin snapped.

"I'm looking for something. I'm not trying to upset you," Tommy explained, still searching for Ryder's number.

"Well, pipe it down a notch," Kevin said, slamming the door.

"Eat a dick," Tommy mumbled to himself.

He knew not to disrespect his pops. He was known for putting hands and feet on Tommy when provoked. Tommy finally found the small paper inside his Nike sneakers box. He picked up the house phone and dialed Ryder's number.

"Hello, may I speak to, Ryder?" Tommy greeted, then asked.

"It's me. Who is this?" Ryder replied, unable to place the voice.

"It's Tommy." He closed his eyes trying to figure out what to say next.

"Hey, Tommy! What's going on? How are you?" Ryder asked excitedly.

"I'm fine. I just called to see what was up with you," Tommy nervously said.

"I'm hanging out with Lil' Woo and Scooter. They came over here with this crazy plan," Ryder told him, looking at Lil' Woo and Scooter.

"A plan for what?" Tommy pried.

"To do things that kids like to do?" Ryder nonchalantly replied.

"What's that?" Tommy was curious.

"Cause trouble."

"Explain," Tommy listened intently.

"Oh, they're looking to get into some trouble. They like to steal bikes, break into small houses, and brownstones," Ryder revealed.

"Are you serious?" Tommy asked.

"Damn serious," Ryder assured him.

"Where?" Tommy asked.

"We usually go to the downtown section of Manhattan, to the suburb side of the Bronx. Kids leave all sorts of things out in their backyards," Ryder plainly stated, looking at a bracelet she found in someone's yard.

"How do you steal?" Tommy asked, revealing the fact that he never stole anything in his life.

"It's easy. We find something we like and take it. Bikes are easy. We see one, get on it, and take off. It's that simple," Ryder stated simply.

"What's up with all these questions, man?" Lil' Woo asked after snatching the phone from Ryder.

"Who is this?" Tommy thought it was one of Ryder's family members.

"Lil' Woo," he said in an intimidating tone.

"What's up, homie?" Tommy was secretly pissed that he was there with Ryder.

"Ain't nothing. I hear you asking Ryder all these questions." Lil' Woo hated when people asked a million questions on the phone.

"Yeah, it sounds crazy, but fun," Tommy admitted.

"It's not crazy, but it's definitely fun. Especially, when we get chased by the owners." Lil' Woo half laughed, thinking of a few crazy mishaps.

"You're crazy. Are Chance and Scooter there?" Tommy asked, even though Ryder just told him Lil' Woo, and Scooter was there.

"They're on their way. Why? I mean, Chance is on his way, but Scooter's here already."

"A'ight, I was just asking." Tommy brushed his response off. "Is Ryder around still?" Tommy wondered why she got off the phone.

"Nah, she went to the bathroom. You want me to get her?" Lil' Woo asked, knowing Tommy liked her.

"No, I'm good," Tommy lied. He was dying inside to speak with her.

"You like Ryder, don't you?" Lil' Woo asked out of nowhere.

"What?"

"Don't what me, fool."

"You already know," said Tommy.

"She kind of likes you too," Lil' Woo told him honestly.

"How you know?"

"I know everything," Lil' Woo said like he was all-seeing and knowing.

"Did she tell you that?" Tommy needed to know.

"Yup! She told me yesterday that she thinks you're cute," Lil' Woo said seriously.

"Do you think I got a shot?" Tommy asked sitting up at the end of his mattress.

"If you play it smooth, you'll be okay. Just stay with the crew. Hanging with the crew will give you direct access to Ryder. She's coming back, change the subject."

"A'ight," Tommy said.

"So, are you coming with us or not?" Lil 'Woo asked.

"Yeah, I'm coming. Where should I meet y'all at?"

"Meet us on 125th Street and Lexington Avenue, on the corner by the pizza shop. We're taking a trip out to the Bronx. We're getting some expensive bikes today that got the full hookups. Mags, pegs, double lock brakes, speed increase, and double-spaced handle bars. That's cool with you?" Lil' Woo asked, pretending like he wasn't just talking about Ryder.

"What time?"

"In like twenty minutes," Lil' Woo said.

"I'll be there," Tommy said, then disconnected the call.

Twenty minutes later, Tommy stood waiting for the crew in front of the pizza shop. He was looking around at all the pretty girls and women who walked by him. He loved Harlem. It was so different from Akron. The energy, style, and demeanor were something to adjust to. Life moved at a different pace in New York.

Ryder came around the corner smiling. She walked up to him and gave him a big hug. Then Lil' Woo, Chance, and Scooter rounded the corner next. They all greeted Tommy with a brotherly hug and dapped him up. Chance looked at Tommy's clothes and made a mental note to teach him how to dress New York style. After their greetings, they got on the Six Train and rode until they reached the last stop. They got off at Pelham Bey Parkway. Lil' Woo lead the way towards the rich part of the Bronx. They walked down to White Plains Road.

While they walked, they saw a lot of possible candidates. Although this section wasn't where they were headed, they were tempted to rethink the location. During their walk, Tommy played Ryder close. Out of the whole crew, Tommy was the only one who looked at her as a sex toy. She noticed a few times Tommy attempted to hold her hand. Had they been alone, he probably would have seized her hand. They walked for an hour and a half searching for a good location to steal from. Most of the houses didn't have any personal items out on the porch, in the driveway, in the grass, or out in the open.

Finally, they came across a backyard with four different color mongoose bikes. The bikes were fully equipped with all the bike tools a kid could ask for. The problem was, there were five of them.

"Those bikes are official," Chance said with bug eyes.

"Someone is going to have to piggyback ride," Scooter said.

"I want the black and red one, it has pegs on it. Ryder can ride on the back until we get cleared and then she can steer," Tommy said quickly. His quick thinking landed him in a position to be close to Ryder.

"You guys can go snatch the bikes. I'll wait here until Tommy comes out. Then I'll hop on the back," Ryder confirmed.

Without any objections, the four young men crept inside the backyard. Each one of them chose a bike to their liking and snatched it. It happened so quickly, that no one saw them go in or out of the yard. Tommy was the last one out. Ryder jumped on the back pegs wrapping one arm around Tommy's neck, securing the other across his chest. They took off riding at top speed and slowed down once they were certain they had gotten away. Lil' Woo was in the lead, but kept looking backwards to make sure everybody got away scot-free.

"Now you're officially part of the crew," Ryder whispered.

"Really?" Tommy replied, enjoying Ryder's arms around his neck.

"You smell good," Ryder complimented.

She could tell by the way he was steering the bike that he was getting aroused. Tommy tried his best to steer straight. Several blocks away from the train station was where they decided to switch positions. Tommy was scared to touch her. He didn't want to mistakenly touch her breast. He jumped on the pegs and held her shoulders. He peeked down her shirt a few times.

"You know you're going to be my wife someday," Tommy whispered.

"What?"

Ryder was so shocked, that she lost balance and crashed into a row of trash cans.

"Wow!"

Tommy leaped off the pegs on the back of the bike and rushed to check on Ryder.

"Are you alright?"

"I'm fine. Get back on before they notice I crashed." Ryder dusted herself off and hopped back on the bike trying her best to hide her embarrassment.

"As long as you're alright," Tommy followed suit, acting as if nothing happened.

"I want to suck the shit out of those nice, perky, firm titties you got," Tommy tried his luck.

"How do you know my titties are perky?" Ryder blushed.

"Cause I can see them," Tommy said, refusing to take his eyes off her mounds.

"You nasty," Ryder removed both hands from the bike bars, buttoned up her shirt, then regained control of the bike again.

"That ain't going to stop nothing. I already saw them," Tommy whispered. "You going to let me suck on your titties?"

"Who knows? Maybe."

Ryder was really good at riding bikes. When they made it to the train station, their train was just a few feet away from the main stop. All the guys picked up their bikes, paid the toll, and charged up the flight of steps. Ryder was the first one up there. She held the door open as they loaded up the train cart. Once everyone was on. She let the door go, and they headed back to Harlem. Mission was accomplished.

Chapter 6

It was a Friday evening when Tommy went running out of the house to avoid his father's mouth. He'd just got off the phone with Ryder, she asked him to come over to her aunt's house and hang out. This became a regular thing for them. Ever since he reached home base with Ryder, they seemed to become each other's shadows. When he came home from school, he scattered all his books around and did all his homework for the weekend. He made a few phone calls, then went to see his woman. He was strung out over Ryder to the highest degree. He walked several blocks down from his house and made it to Ryder's house in five minutes flat.

"Who is it?" Ryder's aunt Diana yelled from the other side of the door.

"It's Tommy," he answered.

"What you want white boy?" Diana playfully asked, looking through the peep hole.

"Is Ryder home?" Tommy asked nicely.

"Yeah, she's here," Diana said, opening the door.

"Hello, Ms. Diana," Tommy greeted as he entered the house.

"Go on, she's in her room," Diana told him, then walked to the kitchen to finish cooking.

"What's up baby girl?" Tommy busted into Ryder's room smiling from ear to ear.

"It's been six months now," Ryder stated looking deep into Tommy's sexy eyes.

"Six months?" Tommy was confused about what she was referring to.

"Six months since the day you whispered in my ear about sucking on my tits," Ryder said, thinking about their first bike ride.

"Oh, you're talking about that. Yeah, I remember," Tommy said smiling.

"Yeah, that's what I'm talking about. I remember when I actually let you do it," Ryder said thinking back to that special day.

"I was scared to death," Tommy admitted.

"Yes, you were."

"I was talking plenty of trash back then, but I can back it up now," Tommy challenged, then grabbed her right titty.

"Hell no! Now you be trying to suck milk out my nipples. You be driving me crazy," Ryder admitted.

"What about my pipe game?" Tommy questioned. He looked into her face for any signs of laughter or regret. He saw none.

"What about it?" Ryder asked, looking him dead in the eyes.

"Is it good?" Tommy asked. He wanted to hear her honest opinion concerning their sex life.

"It's pretty good. If it wasn't, you would know by now," Ryder told him. She liked how he made her feel, and he made her think about their future.

"How?" Tommy asked, wondering if she was trying to save his feelings.

"I would tell you, or I would just stop giving myself to you," Ryder said truthfully.

"You would go cold turkey on me?" Tommy questioned with a raised brow.

"No, I would completely stop. Going cold turkey would only be a temporary thing. It would be for a short while and then pick back up. But once I stop, that means you dead on the pussy." Ryder didn't sugarcoat anything.

"So, tell me this, did you know you were going to give me some from day one?"

"I knew from the moment I saw you. I told myself you were one white boy I wouldn't mind crushing," Ryder smiled.

"You a freak." Tommy shook his head and smirked, then leaned in for a kiss. "So, next time we crush, are you going to do that for me?" Tommy asked, trying to sneak a question in about her giving him oral sex.

"Do what?" Ryder asked confused. She wasn't a mind reader and she didn't have the slightest clue to what he was talking about.

"That rooftop thing?"

"What roof top thing?"

"You know, roof these nuts in your mouth." Tommy laughed.

"I'll roof your nuts alright," Ryder said shoving him backwards on her pillow.

"Seriously though, can I get some head the next time?" Tommy asked again.

"I don't know. It depends." Ryder was the type of person that liked doing things on her time and not a minute before.

"Depends on what?" Tommy pressed. "My dick?"

She laughed. "Hold on, here comes Lil' Woo. My aunt must have let him in. I didn't hear anyone knock. Did you?"

"Nope," Tommy replied, getting off her bed to greet Lil' Woo.

He wanted to see if Chance and Scooter were with him. He didn't see or hear anyone else. So, he waited until Lil' Woo came into the room.

"What's up my dude?" he asked, walking into the bedroom. He shook Tommy's hand, kissed Ryder on the cheek, and gave her a light wind hug.

"Ain't nothing. We just chilling," Tommy said kind of pissed Lil' Woo came over. It was bad enough that Ryder's aunt was in the house, but now he was there too.

"You sure? I hope I didn't interrupt anything between you two love birds," he asked, looking around the bedroom. He felt like he just messed up their little flow.

"We just chilling," Ryder told Lil' Woo. She gave him a weird look.

"I won't stay too long. I only dropped by to give you guys these tickets," Lil' Woo said, reaching into his top coat pocket. He pulled out two pink and purple cards.

"Tickets for what?" Ryder asked excitedly.

She knew Lil' Woo had the right connections in the street to get anything. Even though he was younger than them, his street clout was on the high rise.

"For the Magic Johnson Theater that just open up on 125th Street," Lil' Woo told them.

"I bought it as a belated birthday gift since I didn't get you right on your birthday."

"I thought the tickets were sold out," Ryder said jumping to her feet and examining them.

"Are you sure there real?"

"They better be. All that lunch money I spent on them," Lil' Woo teased. "They're real. I got them from Chance's brother."

"From Mitch? They got to be real then. He don't play no games," Ryder said, still looking at them. "Oh shit, these tickets are for tonight."

"That's right," Lil' Woo confirmed.

"So, who's coming with me?" Ryder asked, looking back and forth at Lil' Woo, then Tommy.

"That's for you and Tommy only," Lil' Woo answered.

"Tommy, do you want to come?" Ryder asked, hoping he'd say yes.

"Yeah, I'll go with you?" Tommy nodded a silent thank you to Lil' Woo.

"What time does the show start?" Tommy asked Ryder.

"It starts at ten o'clock. You sure your dad won't mind?" Ryder asked skeptically.

"Fuck him!" Tommy dismissed his father. "I don't give a shit about what he thinks. Shit, ever since my mother passed away, he's been on some real verbal abusive shit. All he does is drink. He won't even notice I'm gone. As a matter of fact, don't you have a bottle of vodka in here somewhere?"

"It's in my Prada shoebox," Ryder replied.

"Can I get it?" Tommy asked.

"What, you want to drink before the show?" Ryder was confused.

"Hell no. I want to give it to my pops. This way once he's drunk, I'll know for sure I'll be good to go," Tommy said.

"Alright, before you leave to get ready you can get it," said Ryder.

"I can get it, huh?" Tommy said, grabbing his private area.

"Okay, that's my que to go," Lil' Woo said, turning around to walk out of the bedroom.

"Thank you for looking out homie," Ryder said to Lil' Woo.

"No problem, anything for the homies," Lil' Woo said, then walked out.

"Oh, by the way, that'll be three racks a piece. Have my money by midnight," Lil' Woo told them with a straight face.

"What?" Tommy yelled.

"Just kidding." Lil' Woo laughed.

Tommy walked towards the bedroom door, then closed and locked it. He wasted no time snatching Ryder's shirt, bra, and shorts off. He turned her around and bent her over. Quickly, he dropped his pants and underwear, then rammed his manhood into her soft spot. He pounded his girth in and out of her mercilessly. Softly smacking her butt, careful not to be too loud since Ryder's aunt was in the house. Ryder started moaning, loving every second of their sexcapade. She allowed him to place his thumb in her butt hole while he worked her soft spot. This created an overwhelming pleasure. When they were done, Tommy tried to place his manhood into her mouth. But she warned him it would never happen after it came out of her soft spot. She laughed at his annoyance as he pulled his boxers and pants back up and put his manhood away.

****

Later the same night, they went to the show, and it was overcrowded. By the time they got in, the show had already started. Tommy thanked her for inviting him and for giving him that vodka to give his dad. The entire night they held hands and absorbed each other's energy. It was evident that Tommy didn't just like Ryder, he was head over heels in love with her. His heart and mind didn't have room for anyone else. They had officially become a couple. At the end of the show, Tommy and Ryder shared their life goals and discovered this was something else they had in common. They both wanted to be lawyers. But not just any kind of lawyer. Big-time successful lawyers.

Chapter 7

A few years passed by since Tommy and Ryder became a single unit. In the beginning, everything was peaches and cream. They were both in high school with the same plans and mindset for college. Their goals were to be the best lawyers that ever step foot in a courtroom. However, as time went on, Ryder began to take a closer look at her life. College was very expensive and she couldn't afford it. Her money was scarce, and her family lived on a very tight budget. Her goals began to fade away. The street life began to consume her. Ryder was hanging around females who sold their bodies for a living. These girls always had stacks of cash in their pockets.

Ryder was observing their lifestyle with an open mind, and she'd become addicted to sex. Tommy wasn't enough to satisfy her sexual needs anymore. Although she would never tell him this to his face, it was indeed a true fact. She did love Tommy, but she knew she would have to let him go. She would rather leave him alone than stay and hurt him. She no longer craved the dream of becoming a big-time lawyer. That dream went out the window once her aunt died, and she had to fend for herself. The streets became her everything. She began to hang with Lil' Woo more than ever. Mostly because he allowed her to stay at his house. His mother didn't care about anything he did, as long as he kept money coming into the fold. His mother was content with that and never required anything else from him. So, she found a home in his bed.

Normally, they'd meet at the bus stop to ride to school, but for the past four days, Ryder was a no show. She was drifting away from school, and she stopped answering his calls. She sent all his calls straight to voicemail. Tommy tried to locate her and learned that she was staying at Lil' Woo's house. Each time he tried to reach her there, he was told either she just left, or she hasn't come by yet. So, he walked around the neighborhood looking for her. He asked a few people and it just so happened, she'd just left the block of 125th street and was heading down Madison Avenue.

Quickly he rushed to Madison Avenue. He spotted her several blocks away. She was walking slowly like she had the weight of the world on her shoulders. He yelled out her name a few times and watched her turn around to look, but she didn't see him. He ran down the block to catch up with her. When he did, he softly tapped her on her shoulder. He watched her slowly turn around with a sad expression on her face.

"Baby, what's up?" Tommy asked, immediately extending his arms out to her for a hug.

"Tommy, hey babe," Ryder replied, softly diving into his arms, kissing him on his right cheek.

"Ryder where have you been? I've been going crazy trying to reach you. What's going on with your aunt? She doesn't answer the phone or the door anymore," Tommy rambled, trying to gain an understanding of her absence.

"I've been at my little brother's house," Ryder said.

"Who's your brother?"

"Lil' Woo."

"I called there a bunch of times. Lil' Woo never said you were there," Tommy looked Ryder in the eyes. He could see that she was in pain, and had been crying.

"I didn't feel like talking. My aunt passed away," Ryder divulged, then started crying again.

Tommy pulled her into his arms and held her tight as he could. It pained him deeply inside to see her cry.

"I'm sorry, Ryder. I didn't know. I've been worried sick about you. I can't believe no one told me. Lil' Woo, Chance, or Scooter."

"They probably didn't know what to say. They loved my aunt too. I was going to invite you to the service, but it was small and disrespectful. Like, no one showed up for her. No friends or other family members. No one except Lil' Woo and Chance. They helped pay for the services. I miss my aunt so bad." Ryder broke down again.

"It's going to be alright," Tommy assured her.

"No, it's not!"

"Why do you say that?" Tommy asked.

He had no idea what she was going through. He understood the pain of losing a loved one, but he had no idea what was going on.

"Nothing will be the same ever again," Ryder said, releasing her grip around his neck.

"What do you mean?"

"Tommy my life is in shambles."

Tommy tried his best to control his heartache as it beat erratically in his chest. Tommy looked around the area. There wasn't much around, and Madison Avenue was filled with mostly gift shops, tailor shops, and fabric centers. He saw a park with a few benches inside it.

"Let's go have a seat in the park and talk."

"Alright, we can do that," Ryder replied.

Tommy grabbed her hand and silently walked close to her until they made it to the park bench. He tried to figure out what she meant; she was talking sideways. He wanted to know her inner thoughts. He didn't like seeing her in this manner. He held his peace until they arrived at the benches.

"I have no place to live. My aunt is dead. I have no money, and I don't know what to do about school," Ryder said placing her head in both hands. Then laid down on his lap.

"Damn, I don't know what to say. What's going on with your other family members?" Tommy asked.

"They're all dead to me."

"What about all the money you made from all the things we've been stealing?"

"I didn't save nothing. I didn't foresee this happening. I spent most of it on my aunt. I only have crumbs left," Ryder said softly.

"What did Lil' Woo and the crew say?" Tommy asked.

"They will do all they can to help me. Lil' Woo has a plan, but hasn't revealed it to me yet. He wants to step up our game, but I don't have the energy to continue doing jooks. We're not little kids no more. If we get caught. We're going to do some serious time. I'm not a fan of the jail thing," Ryder admitted.

"Is there anything else you can do?"

"There is."

"What is it?" Tommy ran his finger through her hair, trying his best to keep her calm.

"I've been hanging out with some females from Lil' Woo's building. They have this circle of renegades."

"What the hell is a renegade?"

"It's a bunch of girls who get money by sticking together, and turning tricks," Ryder said.

"Turning tricks? Please speak English," Tommy asked confused. The thoughts that came to mind about what he thoughts she was talking about pissed him off.

"I want to be a working girl," Ryder told him.

She sat up and looked in Tommy's face. His eyes filled with tears revealing that he finally understood what she was talking about.

"Are you talking about prostitution?" Tommy needed to make sure he wasn't jumping to conclusions.

"Exactly," Ryder confirmed.

"Oh, hell no." Tommy jumped off the bench like a scorpion stung his leg.

"Ain't no woman of mine going to be out here on these streets selling her ass."

"Tommy that's just it," Ryder cried again. "I have no other choice. I have no other outlet. I watch all these girls splurge off of tricks, and I have nothing. I have to make a power move."

"What about college? What about being a lawyer?" Tommy was struggling to accept Ryder's decision. "You can't do this to me. You can't do this to us. I love you. We can make it. Just give me some time to figure it all out."

"College is just a dream for me, and being a lawyer is too. These are dreams that won't come true for me. I have to deal with reality. My reality shows me that I have to get on my feet immediately," Ryder said seriously.

"I ain't trying to hear that," Tommy snapped. "I can't have no woman of mine giving herself away to random men."

"My decision is final. My mind is already made up," Ryder said standing up to face him. "Give me another outlet."

"You're laying all this on me at once." Tommy scratched his head and paced back and forth trying to come up with an alternate strategy for Ryder.

"I need something, Tommy," Ryder said, watching his frustration grow.

She wasn't trying to hurt him. This entire situation isn't about him. She was heading towards the life of another black girl who was lost in this world. She reached out for Tommy's hand.

"Give me something," she said in a low, desperate, and bitter tone.

"My mind is racing," Tommy said, with pain building up in his chest.

"Well, my heart is racing," Ryder said, looking away from Tommy. Her pain was enormous and unbearable.

"I can't accept that Ryder," Tommy mumbled. "What about your credit? Did you ever touch your credit?"

"My credit is depleted. Someone ran my credit up when I was a little kid. Long before I even knew what credit was. There's a debt there that's outrageous. A figure that would take a lifetime to clear," she said.

"Who did that to you?" Tommy asked.

"My parents were the only ones who had access to my information. So, it was one, or both of them." Ryder shrugged.

"Fuck it. We're stepping our game up. We'll start robbing people we know got it like that. Shit, Chance was just talking about making some real money. All those petty jooks we've been doing are in the past. Now we can step it up," Tommy concluded.

Ryder didn't look convinced. "I don't know about all that. We can talk about it later. Let's go for now."

Tommy nodded. "We'll figure something out."

Chapter 8

Tommy created a slick path as he paced back and forth at the park on 124th Street and Madison Avenue. The smell of pork bacon overwhelmed his nose and made him cough. The entire area was crammed packed with different vendors selling all sorts of different food items. He kept both hands clasped behind his back. This was the only way to keep from punching one of the walls close by.

"I'm not sure I've ever seen you this pissed," Chance said looking at Tommy awkwardly.

"I've been hearing so many rumors about Ryder it's killing me," Tommy snapped.

"But what are you so mad about?"

"Ryder is living with Lil' Woo, correct?" Tommy was pissed.

"That's correct, but you already knew that," Chance stated, with squinted eyes.

"Are they fucking?" Tommy blurted.

"Definitely not," Chance doubted.

"What makes you so sure of that?" asked Tommy.

"They're closer than blood relatives."

"That doesn't answer the question."

"None of us has ever smashed Ryder," Chance said defensively.

"Why not?" Tommy asked looking Chance in the eyes like he was an enemy.

"It's against the brother and sister code," Chance admitted.

"What damn code is that?"

"The code we all agreed on years ago. Long before you came into the picture, we as a crew, vowed to love, cherish, and protect each other. Ryder was bound to be off-limits to us all. None of us so much as ever touched her, kissed her, or tried having sex with her."

"What the fuck is he talking about?" Tommy asked Scooter who sat on a nearby bench just listening.

"What he's telling you is real talk," Scooter said walking up to Tommy.

"We allowed you to deal with her because it was apparent you both had feelings for each other. Plus, you weren't part of the code. So, it doesn't apply to you. But it applies to Lil' Woo and he would never break his code for nothing or no one," Scooter said.

"Look me in my face and tell me straight up that she ain't screwing him."

"Brother he ain't screwing her," Scooter said. He placed his hands on Tommy's shoulder. "He really not."

"Alright, I'll take your word," Tommy said. He looked upward towards the sky. "I just kept hearing so much bullshit that it's getting to me."

"Ryder is in a fucked up situation, but we got her back. You got to take it easy," Chance said honestly.

"Why are we here?" Tommy asked.

"Lil' Woo asked us to meet him at this place. He has some type of power move he wants to make that will set the crew straight for a while," said Scooter.

"Another jook?" Tommy asked, taking a deep breath.

At one point in his life, he loved doing petty jooks with his crew, but life changes people, and time changes everything. Tommy looked around at Scooter and Chance. This lifestyle wasn't for him. It interfered with everything he wanted to do. Living a criminal lifestyle went against his principles and morals. It went against the bar code. If they were planning to hit a jook this would be the last one for him.

He took a deep breath. Slowly, he looked around. New York wasn't for him anymore. And although the love of his life was here, he knew she was living that crazy lifestyle she spoke about. She might not be sexing Lil' Woo, but everyone else in Harlem is getting a piece of that.

"Okay, guys keep it one hundred. I can handle the truth. Is she out hoeing?" Tommy asked.

"Finally, your dumb ass asked the right question," Chance said.

"That's a helluva question," Scooter replied.

"Well, is she?" Tommy asked, losing his patience.

"Homie, that ain't our business to tell. You got to ask Ryder that question," Chance said honestly.

"We talked about it before," Tommy said, turning his head. He looked directly at Lil' Woo coming towards them. "Here comes Lil' Woo now."

"Where?" Chance asked turning around. He saw Lil' Woo walking fast towards them. He nodded his head in acknowledgment of Lil' Woo's presence.

"What's up fellow?" Lil' Woo spoke, walking up to the crew.

He gave everyone handshakes. Then looked at Tommy and felt like something was off. The energy was so negative he picked up on it right away. Being in the street made you aware of certain energy people give off when they're mad.

"Ain't nothing. What's good?" Scooter asked quickly.

"Everything is everything," Lil' Woo said, still looking at Tommy. "What's up with you, homie? How have you been?"

"Nothing much. I've been worrying like hell over Ryder. Where is she?" Tommy asked looking in the direction Lil' Woo just came from. He saw that she was nowhere in sight.

"She's home taking care of some business," Lil' Woo said respectfully.

"What kind of business?" Tommy asked.

"Personal business," Lil' Woo said sensing Tommy was frustrated.

He knew Tommy was missing her like crazy, but he had some real money shit he needed to talk to everyone about so they could get to it.

"Man, I haven't seen her in a while, and I got to ask you something," Tommy said, nearing his breaking point.

"Ask me what?" Lil' Woo said.

"You fucking Ryder?" Tommy asked flat out. He needed to know the truth.

"What?" Lil' Woo said, getting mad. He couldn't believe Tommy just asked him that.

"Are you fucking Ryder?" Tommy asked seriously, looking Lil' Woo dead in the eyes. He was checking for signs of discomfort. He didn't sense any.

"My sister?" Lil' Woo said, ready to snap on Tommy for asking a dumb-ass question like that.

"She ain't your real sister," Tommy said.

"She's more my sister than she could ever be your girl. We have a code, and the code is for Ryder. No one touches her. The only reason you fucking her is because I allowed it," Lil' Woo clarified.

"What'chu you mean you allowed it? That's my woman," Tommy said stepping forward.

"Homie, I ain't about to go back and forth with you over my sister. No, I ain't fucking her, but I'm the least of your worries. She's my homie. There's nothing shaking between her and me. She could be butt naked in my bed with her ass pressed on my dick rock hard, and I still wouldn't violate the code," Lil' Woo protested.

"I just needed to know straight up, that's all. But, anyway, what you had us meet here for?" Tommy asked.

"I got us one of the sweetest jooks in the world," Lil' Woo said.

"Doing what?" Chance asked excitedly.

"You always come through with something," Scooter said.

"Tell us what's the deal," Tommy said, ready to get it over with.

"I got us a sweet jooks uptown. This young boy just came up. He won some type of lawsuit money and now he's splurging like crazy. The nigga stays high and drunk all the time. The problem is he's always with someone. I believe the person with him might be gripped up. Homie got mad platinum, gold, and ice. The nigga, be selling weed too. It's a crazy come-up. The dude doesn't know none of us," Lil' Woo said.

"What's his name?" Chance asked.

"His name is Creepy," Lil' Woo said. "He's a bit older than us, but he ain't got no heart or backbone."

"Never heard of him," Scooter said.

"I never heard of him either. I'm game," Chance said, agreeing to ride out.

"I'm down," Scooter said.

"You guys think this shit is a game, huh?" Tommy asked.

"Are you in or not?" Lil' Woo asked.

"I'm in," Tommy said. "When are we going to do this?" Tommy asked shaking his head. He was still thinking about Ryder. "Is Ryder coming along?"

"We doing this tonight, and no, she ain't popping on this trip. She got to handle her own business," Lil' Woo said, starting to get pissed at Tommy.

****

Later that same night, the crew met up dressed in all black. They looked like they were ready to get into some drama. They made their way uptown. When they came to the set location, they found their target with his homie drinking and smoking in the lobby of his building. The four men moved in quickly on the two targets. They roughed them up and made them go inside a staircase. The crew found a gun on the targets. Then they got bulks of cash from them, took their diamond rings, and got all of the platinum chains they wore. It was a major come-up for the crew.

Chapter 9

Far too much time passed since Tommy last saw Ryder. Even after their last jooks, he still hadn't touched base with her. He was ready to start a new route in life, and he need to get out of New York. He needed to see his woman and talk to her. So, he went to Lil' Woo's house early in the morning.

"Who is it?" a voice came from the other side of the door.

"Tommy," he yelled waiting for the door to open.

Lil' Woo opened the door.

"Where is she?" Tommy asked refusing to back down. He stepped forward inside the doorway and paused. He glanced inside and saw no sign of Ryder's presence.

"Where is who?" Lil' Woo asked opening the door further. When he looked at Tommy, he knew he didn't know Ryder was out in the streets selling ass.

"Where's Ryder?" Tommy exploded in a frenzy. He wanted his woman. He was worried sick about her wondering why she hadn't made contact with him.

"She ain't here." Lil' Woo told him truthfully. He wasn't about to expose Ryder's personal business to him.

"Man, tell me where she is?" Tommy said looking down into Lil' Woo's eyes. Tommy was on a thousand.

"I don't know," Lil' Woo said turning his face into a frown. Lil' Woo couldn't believe Tommy was so pussy whipped over Ryder. He was acting like a mad man.

"Are you serious?" Tommy asked skeptically, thinking he could be telling the truth. His beef wasn't with Lil' Woo, it was with Ryder.

"She left out early this morning," Lil' Woo said, stepping backwards, and crossing his arms.

"Did she say anything before she left?" Tommy was concerned and needed some type of information.

"She don't tell me nothing," Lil Woo told Tommy flat out. "She don't ever tell me jack shit. She comes and goes as she pleases." He shrugged as if Tommy was overreacting.

"Why not?" Tommy pressed, unwilling to accept what Lil' Woo told him.

"I ain't her babysitter," Lil' Woo snapped.

"But she's your homie." Tommy knew Lil' Woo would be the main one, if anyone, to know Ryder's whereabouts.

"I ain't my homies keeper," Lil' Woo said making sure Tommy understood this. Deep inside Lil' woo was getting pissed.

"Do you have any idea where she might've gone?" Tommy asked sounding extremely worried. Desperate. He stared Lil' Woo down hard. "You supposed to be my homie too!" he said sincerely. He believed real homies didn't lie to each other, and neither did they keep each other in dark about serious situations.

"You are my homie," Lil' Woo said, placing his hand on Tommy's shoulder. "You got to chill out though."

"You don't act like it," Tommy said, looking straight through Lil' Woo's eyes. He saw nothing but pure evil.

"What's all this about?" Chance asked. He didn't like the energy Tommy came in the house with, but he understood it.

"It's about Ryder," Tommy said, turning to Chance quickly.

"I haven't seen her in weeks," Tommy said.

"This is the only place I know she'd be at, but yet she ain't never here."

"How is this my fault?" Lil' Woo asked while walking past Chance and winking his eye. It was a signal telling him not to expose Ryder's secret.

"I never said it was your fault," Tommy announced. "It ain't no one fault. I just want to see and talk to Ryder."

"Listen, your welcome to wait here for Ryder if you want to. Come inside and close the door behind you, homie," Lil' Woo told him, as he reached for an apple off the coffee table and started eating it.

"Thanks," Tommy said.

He stepped all the way inside, closed the door, and locked it.

"What's up Chance?" Tommy asked, checking the homie's expression. No one seemed excited to see him.

"Cooling," Chance said calmly. He understood that being left in the dark about Ryder made him feel a certain way.

"What's popping, Scooter?" Tommy asked, turning his attention towards him. He noticed there was a big blunt in his hand.

"Nothing Brody," Scooter said sarcastically. He was laying back watching the show. He found the situation amusing.

"What ya'll been up to?" Tommy asked out loud to no one in particular. He was trying to make conversation.

"Getting this money," Chance said, slapping a respectful right hand on Tommy's shoulder.

"You missed out on a few jooks," Scooter said, placing his blunt on the coffee table in front of him. He rose up and walked towards the living room closet. Once inside, he retrieved his metal football-printed lighter out of his pocket and went back to grab his blunt off the table.

"What jooks?" Tommy said seriously. The last one they did set him straight, but another one would have put him on top.

"Ain't no one tell him about the suitcase man?" Scooter asked, looking around for answers.

"You were supposed to tell him," Lil' Woo chimed in.

"Oh shit! Man, I smoke too much," Scooter said, feeling embarrassed.

"Stop mixing that K2 shit in your weed," Chance said. "That duce is frying your brain."

"You said Tommy passed on the jooks," Lil' Woo put him on the spot, then smirked. He realized that Tommy didn't flunk out on their mission. Shit, he never even knew about the setup.

"Y'all dudes is tripping. What jooks, and what the fuck is duce?" Tommy said sitting down on the couch. He realized that they had been keeping him in the dark on mad shit. But it was alright. His time in New York was coming to an end anyway. All this just put a stamp on his final decision to head down South and start a new life. These guys weren't his real homies.

"We caught a couple of racks off this retarded red neck that owns a jewelry store in Brooklyn," Lil' Woo told him.

"When was this?" Tommy asked.

"A couple of days ago," Chance said looking at Tommy. He thought Tommy flaked out on them, but it's obvious that wasn't the case. Scooter was doing a lot of bullshit lately.

"Duce is some new weed that came out. The shit is thirty times more potent than regular weed. Like, the shit be making people have episodes," Lil' Woo said.

"That shit be making muthafuckas trip out," Chance added.

"This fool ass nigga keeps mixing that shit with real weed," Lil' Woo snapped and looked at Scooter. "You a dumb ass fool."

"Fuck you!" Scooter said raising his middle finger real high.

"Let me see the duce," Tommy asked.

"I got some right here," Scooter said, digging inside his pocket. "This shit right here will help you get straight high grades on that lawyer shit you on. You'll pass the bar with flying colors," Scooter said teasing Tommy. He passed him a container that looked like a hockey puck. Tommy grabbed the container and opened it. The raw smell made him lean back.

"This shit smells wicked."

"That's, that fire," Scooter defended, lighting his blunt, then took a long hard tote.

The potency of the duce inside the blunt was evident and Scooter wobbled backwards. He could barely walk off of one long pull. Once he sat down, he started mumbling something under his breath about Ryder being a prostitute, but his words were more of a slur and weren't clear to understand.

Tommy stayed there for a couple of hours waiting for Ryder and ended up playing NBA live on the XBOX. He completely lost track of time. While playing someone knocked on the apartment door. He watched Lil' Woo jump up, running towards the front door to answer it.

A few seconds later, Ryder came walking inside the bedroom smelling like pure sex. Everyone in the house could smell it. It was so strong that it overwhelmed Tommy's nose and caused him to sneeze. Ryder stood there staring at him.

"Hey, Tommy. What are you doing here?"

Tommy put the remote control down and watched as everyone inside the room left. They needed some privacy. When Scooter walked out, he told Ryder she needed to tell Tommy the truth. Tommy heard him loud and clear.

"What's going on?" Tommy asked.

"What do you mean?" Ryder replied sadly.

"I've been worried sick as shit about you."

"Why?" Ryder asked. She had this; *I don't give a fuck* aura about her. It accompanied the ripe smell coming off her ass.

"What is wrong with you? Are you on drugs or something? Why do you smell like sex?" Tommy pried.

"There's nothing wrong with me. I don't use drugs, and I smell like sex because I've been fucking my ass off," Ryder admitted.

"Wow! So that's the route you decided to go?" Tommy asked painfully.

"I told you already that I was," Ryder said putting her head down shamefully.

She started removing her clothes, acting like Tommy was nothing to her. But deep down inside, her heart was bleeding. She knew she had to let him go.

"No, you told me you were thinking about it. I'm your man and you're treating me like I'm a sucker." Tommy was hurt but Ryder's actions and decisions.

"It's not like that. I'm hurting for money. I have nothing," Ryder said.

"I'm leaving New York," Tommy revealed.

"Where are you going?" Ryder asked.

"I'm going to college in Atlanta. I can't take this New York shit anymore. I'm going to law school. I wanted you to come with me, but I see you've changed your goals in life. When I leave out that door today, you won't see me again... ever." Tommy's heart broke with every word.

"I guess I have to let you go then," Ryder said. Her eyes filled up with tears.

Tommy turned and left.

Chapter 10

Leaving New York turned out to be a little harder than Tommy expected. The people he considered as friends and family all stayed behind. He stood on the curb with the yellow cab door wide open. He glanced up and down the street taking in the surrounding area for a last memory. He looked backwards and saw kids crossing the street on their way to school. He took in a deep breath and held it a few seconds before releasing New York City's morning aromas.

"I'm ready whenever you are," Felix the cab driver said. He slapped the hood of the cab, then hopped in the back seat.

"I'm ready," Tommy said, after securing his door.

"So, where are you headed?" Felix asked trying to make conversation.

In his twenty-seven years of being a taxi driver, there hadn't been too many customers who turned out to be friendly people. Tommy was one out of the few.

"Down south," Tommy said. He was trying to adjust himself so that he could be comfortable for the little ride.

"I'm talking about where you want me to take you?" Felix asked again. He knew something heavy was on this man's mind.

"La Guardia Airport," Tommy said while looking backwards as the cab started moving. He told Ryder that he was going to be leaving to catch an early flight. He warned her that once he left, he wouldn't be back. He told her the time his flight left and sent her a text message letting her know he was leaving. Something deep inside Tommy was hoping that Ryder, and the crew, were going to stop him from leaving. Yet, there was a part of him that knew no one was going to show up for him.

"Good ole' La Guardia. I use to work in that airport. I got fired because I kept stealing all the rich folk's luggage." Felix laughed. "Yup, I use to steal before I made an honest living. I hated seeing all those rich folks with expensive unnecessary things. Like, one rich lady had an ostrich as an emotional companion. Who in the hood would buy an ostrich for emotional support?"

"Nobody that I know." Tommy held small talk, but his mind was elsewhere.

"Exactly!" Felix snapped like he was having a flashback.

Tommy turned completely around in his seat, scanning the block for Lil' Woo's car or any one of the crew's cars. He saw nothing. He scanned the side looking for Ryder who should've been running to catch him before he left.

There wasn't one crew member in sight. The same people he called his crew, were the same ones who didn't show any loyalty. Not one person came to see him off. Some friends they were. He was glad he made this decision. If he hadn't, he would have never figured out that Lil' Woo and his crew were never really his friends.

"An ostrich. Like who does that?" Tommy asked while entertaining the conversation.

"Only the damn rich," Felix said while pulling up to a red light.

"So, you're going down south, huh?"

"Yea."

"For the girls?" Felix asked knowing that's usually what most men shoot out to Atlanta for.

"Nah, I'm going to school," Tommy said sounding like a complete square.

"What school?" Felix asked wondering if he was heading to his old place of graduation.

"Atlanta City College," Tommy told him.

"You should've just said you were going for the girls. That college ain't nothing but a huge pussy attraction. There are more girls on that compound than there are men in prison," Felix said honestly.

"How do you know, old man?"

"Old man?" Felix repeated. "Young fella, I went to that same school. Look right here." Felix pointed to a group picture. All the people in there had ACC shirts on that stood for Atlanta City College. "This is my graduation picture from that school."

"I thought you were bullshitting me," Tommy said while leaning forward to get a closer look.

"No bullshit. Class of 1976," Felix said smiling. He pulled his driver's hat down over his forehead.

"Damn, you had hair back then." Tommy laughed.

"Leave my bald head alone," Felix replied laughing.

"Let's get out of here. I never want to see this place again. It was a bad move that my parents made to come here. New York is not what it's cracked up to be. Shit, you can't even find real friends here. I hope my new location turns out to be better. I know it's going to be hard," Tommy said sadly.

"New York is good for quick come-ups and visiting. It's not a good place to live if you ain't rich. If you're looking for a real change in your life Atlanta is the home of change. Now is a good time to pick up and go. Around this time in Atlanta, school sessions are just heating up."

"Anything is better than New York right now," Tommy said agreeing with Felix.

Tommy saw the George Washington Bridge coming up. The airport was only twenty minutes away. He stared at the New York scenery. It was officially time to let go.

Twenty minutes later, Felix pulled into the parking lot of the airport. Luckily for Tommy, he was traveling very light. His one bag was small enough to fit inside the baggage container above the seats on the plane. Once he paid Felix, he walked inside the airport. His heart started beating fast when he stepped inside the airport. There were so many people leaving New York it was sickening. He scanned the flight monitor, then pulled out his tickets and checked the listings. He walked over to Flight Deck 47. Although he was ready to leave, he yearned for Ryder's presence. He secretly prayed and held out hope that Ryder would show up.

He found himself a seat, removed his portable laptop, and logged into his social media account. He shared the news on Facebook that he was boarding his flight at LaGuardia tunnel, number forty-seven in another hour. Once he was done, he checked Ryder's page. The green light meant she was active. Tommy waited for a few minutes to see if she would comment on his media message. However, her green light turned red without a response. He clicked onto Ryder's other media sites. All of them went out simultaneously. He slammed his laptop shut and looked around, hoping he didn't alarm anyone.

His loading dock had already started letting people on. The line for 47 was long, so he stood right beside a young boy who was playing Spiderman on his hand game. He looked back and forth between the game and the main entrance. His mind drifted off to Ryder as he hoped she came storming through the entrance and begged him to stay. But it wasn't going to happen, so he said a silent prayer for her.

Tommy slowly handed over the flight ticket and watched the man snatch the snub part off before handing it back. Slowly, he walked down the passenger's flight tube. He stopped and turned around one last time until the flight attendants ordered him onto the plane. He watched them shut the corridor doors. At that moment, it was all over.

*****

This was Tommy's first time flying on a plane. He got scared every time the plane experienced a little turbulence while in the air. After he had two drinks the ride became smooth and he was able to relax. During the hour trip over the water, he became nervous. Once that part of the flight was over, he fell asleep for the rest of the ride.

When he finally arrived in Georgia, his heart was pounded a mile a minute. He couldn't believe he'd really made it. The sight from above was amazing. The people were beautiful, and he knew this was the beginning of his long-awaited dream. Once the flight attendants gave the green light, everyone started grabbing their property to leave off the plane.

Tommy was in the first group of people who stormed off of the plane. He was happy to make it to Atlanta unharmed. He refused to let any of his fears interfere with his first-time experience. He crept his way toward the front of the airport. When he stepped outside, he felt like he was on forty-second street in Time Square. The air was so fresh. Immediately he sensed the difference in the air's texture. New York's air was overwhelming and toxic, as opposed to Atlanta's humid, fresh air. He stepped over to the sidewalk and looked at the rows of cabs. He peered at four of them before one of the cabs stopped for him.

"ACC!" Tommy told the cab driver.

"Put everything in the trunk," the cab driver said. He popped the trunk and watched Tommy put his property inside. Then he observed how he quickly got inside the car, took a deep breath, and looked around.

"ACC please," Tommy said again politely.

"Sure pal. What's your beef?" the cab driver asked knowing full well Tommy wasn't from around there.

"What do you mean? I don't understand what you're asking me," Tommy asked curiously.

"What are you going to ACC for?" the cab driver asked while looking through the rearview mirror.

"To get a degree," Tommy said like he was talking to a twelve-year-old child.

"In what?" the cab driver asked ignoring the disrespect.

"Law," Tommy said flatly, turning his attention out the window.

"Oh, you fixing to be a prosecutor? You trying to lock up the black community?" the cab driver inquired sarcastically.

"You're crazy," Tommy shot back.

"Well, good luck," the cab driver said before he fell completely silent.

A little while later, the cab driver pulled into the main campus parking lot. It was crammed packed with cars, bikes, students, and hangouts. Tommy took in the sight, looked at his pass, then found the registration office to sign the remainder of his paperwork for school. Once that was completed, he made his way to his dorm room to set up and unpack.

Chapter 11

Atlanta City College is one of the biggest colleges in the United States. There are ten sections on this campus, each section has four large buildings and two smaller buildings. All the smaller buildings in each section were for freshmen. The bigger buildings were for upperclassmen. Tommy stood directly in front of the college in disbelief. He couldn't believe he'd finally made it. After a few years of law, and a degree, he'll be on his way. Thousands of students were coming and going, and he took it all in while envisioning his future. Some freshmen girl walking by bumped him, knocking him out of his brief trance.

As he took strides towards the administration building, he found a section tour guide. He traced the guide to the building he was looking for, and it just happen to be the building off to his right. It looked like the administration building with the American flag hung high. Once inside, he located the clerk who dealt with new students. The clerk was a small, petite Chinese girl with long black hair and huge glasses. The girl had to look up to see Tommy when he approached her desk.

"How may I help you?"

"My name is Tommy White. I'm here to pick up my cards, my programs, and my books," Tommy said, propping his arms on the countertop. He waited while she flipped through a huge book until she found my cards, then disappeared to the back. When she returned, she had my programs in hand.

"Tommy White?"

"Yes."

"Okay, here's your school identification card, your program card, and your teacher will give you your books when you get there. I see you're going to the law school section, that's a very good career choice," the clerk encouraged him.

"Could you tell me where the law school building is located?"

"It's in the third section," the clerk directed. "Most of your classes will start with the number 3. The number on each section is the first number you see, and the actual classroom is across from the period section. You'll see, first period 101." The clerk stood up and pointed at the card.

"So, this room 101 is my home room, and it's in the first section," Tommy said skeptically.

"That's correct," she confirmed.

"So, the first number is the section, and the number as a whole is the classroom?" Tommy asked scanning his card.

"Yes," she agreed. "Your homeroom class is going to start in five minutes. Don't be late on your first day. Good luck."

"Thank you," Tommy said, rushing out of the administration office.

He glanced around locating the first section, then hustled towards his homeroom class. The moment he found his class, he picked the first open chair he saw and sat down. The teacher walked inside the room moments later without a single word, slamming his suitcase on his desk. He glanced around and recognized two new faces.

"I need someone to handle the introductions," the teacher said.

"I'll take care of it," someone said out of nowhere. "We have two new students in the room. Will the two new students step up to the front and state your name, where you are from, and announce your major?" she asked.

Tommy and the other student got up and walked to the front of the class as they were asked to do. Tommy let the other guy go first.

"My name is, Steward Clipps. I'm from Atlanta, and I'm majoring in studio arts."

Tommy was a little nervous and didn't expect the other guy to be done so soon. All eyes were on him. He announced his information and stated that his major was criminal law. The second he was done talking he hurried back to his seat. As soon as he sat down, another student slid into the empty chair next to his. The guy had a stack of cards in his hand.

"Hey Tommy, here's wreck pass. It's an invitation to the coolest frat party this season," he said, nudging Tommy's shoulder and passing him the card.

"Keep this card and give it to whoever's at the door. If you lose this baby, you won't get in. My name is Steve. I'm your party pusher."

"I don't have time for frat parties," Tommy said.

"Maybe not now, but you will dude. Trust and believe you will," Steve said seriously.

"Are there going to be girls there?" Tommy asked not feeling the energy.

"Shit loads, man," Steve said emphasizing. "It's for us all. Freshmen, middlemen, and seniors. Everyone with a card is invited. There's going to be a lot of bitches there. Don't miss it."

"Cool," Tommy said, accepting his invitation card.

"We're all about to shoot out to our next class. You'll probably be heading to the third section. That's where all the law classes are located," Steve whispered.

"Here's another invitation. Bring a snow bunny with you."

"What's a snow bunny?" Tommy questioned, watching Steve grab his property.

"A white girl," Steve smiled.

"A white girl?" Tommy repeated.

"Man, just bring a bitch with you," Steve whispered inside Tommy's ear so the teacher wouldn't hear him.

"I don't know anyone yet."

"You will, and when you do, bring her with you," Steve assured him, then grabbed his property as the bell rang for the second period.

"Nice to me you man."

Tommy examined the cards briefly as he left out his homeroom class. He walked towards the exit and scanned all the students who passed him by. He noticed a large number of females strutting around, and everyone moved fast.

Once outside, he walked with haste. Tommy found the law school section. It was weird and extremely different compared to the rest of the campus. From the moment he entered the section it was like clouds of silence flooded the area. It was so quiet it seemed like he'd entered another dimension. He saw a waiting line and jumped in it. He found himself bumping people to get in. One girl he bumped gave him a shy smile. Lust was written all over her face. When he said excuse me, the girl nodded her head acknowledging his apology.

"You must be new here," the girl said smiling.

"First day," Tommy replied.

"You're in my class. My name is Debby Wilde," she said, staring at his program card. She extended her right hand to greet him.

"I'm Tommy White. How do you know I'm in your class?" Tommy asked, looking at her weirdly.

"I saw your card. It looks like you're in all my classes except homeroom. That's good."

"Why is that?" Tommy asked. He didn't like people snatching shit from him.

"Because now you have someone to walk with you around campus. Unlike most of us, when we first started. We didn't have any human tour guides." She flipped over the card and saw the frat party invitation. "I see you got an invitation."

"Some dude in homeroom gave it to me," Tommy replied.

"That dude in your homeroom is Steve. Nine times out of ten it's his party. I see you got two. So, who are you bringing? You got a girlfriend already?" Debby teasingly pried.

"You say this like it's the best thing in the world. No, I don't have a girlfriend. I ain't looking for one either," Tommy shot back.

"You don't have to look, they'll find you. Where are you from?" Debby asked.

"New York," Tommy said proudly.

"A New York City slickster in the house," Debby said, twerking her round ass. "I love New York, and I love the men who come from New York even more. I knew you had this hood swag with you."

"What do you mean?" Tommy asked raising an eyebrow.

"I mean, you got swag. A girl like me knows swag when I see it. You ain't one of those pussy soft white boys. I see you," Debby teased.

"Where are you from?" Tommy inquired.

"I'm from the windy city of whores," Debby said flirtatiously.

"Where's that?" Tommy asked, studying her disposition. Just bringing up the word whore made his insides shiver.

"Texas," Debby told him.

Debby knew a sucker when she saw one, but Tommy didn't strike her as a full-blown victim. Dudes from New York City were hipped to women like Debby, who played wolf dressed in sheep's clothing. She sensed a protection issue with Tommy. She felt like Tommy could be geared up to play the male role in her life. What Tommy didn't know is that he just got closer.

Chapter 12

Debby was the first woman on the campus to enter the men's dormitory. She'd always made it her business in life to be up early. She bought that *'get up early'* mind state to ACC which is how she quietly walked through the halls to Tommy's room.

Tap-Tap-Tap.

"Who's there?" Tommy asked, turning over in his bed. He wasn't expecting anyone. No one comes to visit him, so the knock startled him.

"Debby," she answered, pushing open the door, and making her way in.

"Are you ready for the big party?" Debby yelled, knowing he wasn't completely up and ready for nothing.

"What party?" Tommy asked, rolling over in the bed again, looking at the clock on his nightstand.

"The one you got the invitation for when you first started class," Debby said. She thought he'd be up and ready for the day, but he wasn't.

"When is it?" Tommy asked with confusion written all over his face. He didn't have any plans for a party.

"It's tonight," Debby said excitedly.

"I forgot all about that," Tommy admitted groggily.

"Well, at this party is where you'll get to see the real college life," Debby announced, yanking at his bed spread to see if he was naked.

Every day classes were kicking his ass, and he had a full schedule. "I thought this was the real college life," Tommy said sarcastically.

"No, this is college school life. College life starts tonight. Are you going?" Debby asked, faking sadness.

"Probably not," Tommy told her straight up. "I ain't got no energy for a party," Tommy mumbled under his breath.

"What?!" Debby exploded.

"Don't what me. You heard what I said," Tommy shot back. He peeked over his blanket to make sure she didn't set a fire.

"You have to go!" Debby snapped, continuing to pull on his blanket and pillow too.

"Why?" Tommy asked wondering what was so special about a college party.

"I need to get in. You're going to be my pass," Debby let him know.

"Would you stop it?" Tommy snapped, losing patience with her.

"I'll stop if you promise to take me to the party," Debby said flirtatiously, climbing into his bed. She lay next to him and stared into his eyes.

"Wait a second," Tommy snapped, looking at her sideways.

"What?" she snapped back. She saw the confused expression he gave her.

"How did you get into my room?" Tommy asked, looking at the bedroom door.

"The door was open," Debby said honestly.

"I'm from New York. I don't leave doors open," Tommy shot back quickly. That was something he never did in his life.

"Well next time make sure you locked it. All I did was knock on the door. When I turned the door handle your door swung open," Debby said crawling out of the bed and grazing his private area like it was a mistake. It wasn't.

"How did you know where I lived?" Tommy asked while he gained his morning senses back.

"I didn't. I asked about the new guy, and someone pointed me in the right direction. No one knew your name, but they refer to you as the New York guy. You know, it's not like every other person you meet is from New York. You're quite easy to find. Plus, you're the only white boy from New York in law school. Everyone on campus watches the law school kids. So, you're fairly easy to track down," Debby informed him as she walked towards his dresser.

"Why weren't you in class yesterday?" Tommy asked skeptically.

"Money situations. That's why I need to be at this frat party. You're my only way in," Debby admitted.

"Why don't you just take the pass and get out," Tommy suggested like he wasn't interested in her.

"Where is it?"

"It's in the closet in my black leather jacket pocket," Tommy said while rubbing his eyes. He had to get the crust out, it was toying with his vision.

"I'll get it," Debby said, pushing open his closet doors. She scanned the closet for a black leather jacket, retrieved the ticket, and shoved it inside her bra.

"Did you find it?" Tommy asked, trying to see what she was doing.

"I got it," Debby replied.

"So, how is this party going to help you with your money issues?"

"The guys there get high, get drunk, and get horny. Then there's me. I make my money by entertaining them," Debby plainly stated.

"Get horny? What does that have to do with you?" Tommy curiously pried.

"That's when I step in. That's when it's time for me to lie, cheat, steal, and fuck for that almighty dollar," Debby bragged, raising her hand in the air, rubbing her fingers together like there was money in it.

"You're a working girl?" Tommy was visibly shocked at the revelation. He never pegged her to be that type of woman.

"Is that what y'all call it in New York?"

"Basically."

"I'm an opportunist. I do what I gotta do to pay my way through college. Some of us aren't fortunate to have a silver spoon in our mouths. Some of us have to fend for ourselves."

"So, you're a prostitute?"

"I prefer the ward escort. I'm a high-class escort."

Tommy didn't give off any clues to how he felt about escorts, and this was enough to convince her that she'd picked the right fool.

"You're a renegade?"

"We don't use that term at all down here in the south. We refer to ourselves as escorts. Nothing more and nothing less," Debby said with great pride.

"You got a pimp?" Tommy asked, knowing that all whores had pimps, and if there's no pimp involved then the whore normally has a friend looking out.

"There's no need for one, but I do have a secret person in mind to ride along with me."

"Who?"

"You're crazy. It's gotta be something in this Atlanta air."

"Something like what? Are you going to tell me who you got in mind?"

"I got you in mind, but I don't know where you stand."

"Where I stand?"

"Like do you know anything about this lifestyle? Can you fight? Are you a tough guy? Do you know any musical arts?" Debby asked a bunch of questions, and she needed an answer for each one.

"I'm familiar with whores. I ain't no tough guy, and I don't know any martial arts, but I can fight."

"You're perfect," Debby lied. "So, get up! Get ready, eat some breakfast, and start your day. Tonight, we ride out to the party."

"Ride out? I don't have a car. It's not on campus?"

"It's a twice a week show-down party for students who are on campus. The address is on your invitation. Don't worry, I got the wheels. Do you know how to drive?"

"Of course, I just don't have my license yet."

"Great, I'll pick you up, and you can drive us there. I got a GPS in my ride, so don't worry," Debby said aggressively.

*****

Later that night, Debby came to pick him up as promised. She had to text him twice before he came out of his dorm and entered the parking lot. From the moment she saw him walking, she knew she'd picked the right one. She examined his frame as he strolled over to the awaiting car.

Tommy took the steering wheel and followed the GPS directions. The place of venue was a mini-mansion. When they arrived, Tommy got the shock of his life. It wasn't an ordinary party. It was a lingerie party. Men and women were half-naked on the lawn, porch, pool area, front gate, and all over the premises. Titties and ass were everywhere.

After a few hours, Tommy was heavy in the mix. His financial situation was starting to look bad, that is until he helped Debby pull a few tricks. In return, she pushed him some money. She was knocking off several heads at a time.

Most men were super intoxicated, and all she had to do was wait until they passed out. This is how she made extra money. Now she had Tommy to hold her down.

Chapter 13

Tommy looked at his watch. It was time to go to class. He turned the corner that led down the long corridor where Mr. Riverwall advised them to meet up.

"How are you feeling?" Tommy asked Debby as he walked towards the classroom. Today, was their bar exam.

"Nervous," Debby replied, going over a bunch of notes in her hand.

"Is that all?"

"I'm anxious too," Debby smirked.

"And?" Tommy asked leaning his head close to hers.

"Determined."

"Don't feel bad. I have all the same feelings as you, but I'm beyond ready. "Tommy said while pounding on his chest like King Kong."

"How do you think you're going to do?" Debby asked turning to face Tommy.

"I feel an ace coming up," Tommy boasted.

"I don't sense an ace on my behalf, but I definitely feel like something good is going to happen here today," Debby said looking around at the other students.

Tommy smiled. "We studied hard, and bust our asses to take this bar exam. All our grades have been excellent. Don't have a breakdown on me now."

"That's true," said Debby nodding.

"I didn't do too bad on the practice test, so I don't see any reason why I should worry about the real test," said Tommy glancing around at the other students waiting.

"That was only a practice, it wasn't the real deal. Today, it all counts," Debby reminded him as if he wasn't already aware.

"If you can beat the practice test, you should be able to get a high-ranking score on the bar exam." Tommy shrugged. "Have faith in yourself."

"I guess you're right. We've made it this far. Now it's time to move forward in life and pass this bar exam," Debby said seriously, twirling her hair around her finger. "I can't lie. I spoke with a lot of people. Some passed the bar, and others were short by a few points. They all proclaimed the bar exam to be one of the hardest tests they've ever taken."

"Yes, I heard that too, but I refuse to allow someone else's shortcomings to affect me. I'm getting this damn degree today."

"Yes, we're going to get this degree today," Debby agreed.

"What? You sound like you plan on cheating," Tommy said looking around.

"Yeah right," Debby denied.

Tommy gave her a hard stare.

"Hello class, I'm Mr. Riverwall. Could you guys please come with me?" A tall white man asked, after peeking his head out of the classroom into the hall.

Quickly he made a head count. He noticed one student was missing, so, he put a sign up on the door to let anyone who is late know that the law class was testing inside the computer room. The note had the date and time of the exam. If anyone is late, they will have to do the class over.

Debby, Tommy, and the rest of the students taking the test followed Mr. Riverwall down the long quiet corridor. They followed him until they arrived at the main computer lab. At the door, he handed everyone a placement card and ordered everyone to find their names on a desk.

Debby and Tommy were on the other side of the room. There's a total of twenty students taking the bar exam today. The one guy the class was waiting for finally made it. He was lucky because once the testing started, he would have been ass out of luck.

Mr. Riverwall passed out a handful of number two freshly sharpened pencils and wished everyone good luck on the exam. Afterwards, he walked around scanning people's names and passing them booklets. Everyone had a different color booklet. It didn't symbolize anything special, it just let the teacher know which booklet the test came from. The only difference besides the color was the mere fact that the questions were arranged differently. This prevented people from having wandering eyes.

At nine o'clock sharp, the bar exam started. It was so quiet in the room the rumbling of people's stomachs could be heard throughout the class. Everyone was flying through the first several sections of the book. Three hours later, everyone was allowed to pass in their booklets, and take a break. Tommy and Debby went strolling towards the cafeteria room. They grabbed some lunch trays, drinks, and dessert, and sat down in a corner near a window. Once they were done eating, they made their way back to class to finish the exam.

When they arrived, all the other students were waiting at the door for Mr. Riverwall to open the doors back up. Everyone got their same booklets back, took their seat in the same spot, and got back to work. The bar exam lasted all day. It wasn't until after six o'clock p.m. that the teacher finally announced that the test is over. Everyone put their pencils down. He told everyone that the new system for getting test results will allow him to have test scores for everyone in a few weeks.

****

Two Weeks Later…

Everyone who took the bar exam was summoned to Mr. Riverwall's main classroom. They waited outside in the corridor while one person went inside, and another came out. At the other end of the hallway, there were several happy cheers, and a few sympathy cries. Tommy and Debby were next in line. They promised to open up each other's results. Tommy went inside first. After a few minutes he stepped out and Debby stormed inside anxiously. She came right back out and handed her papers to Tommy. They walked down the corridor and exploded with joy because they both passed. She had several points more than him. They hugged and kissed one another on the cheek.

"You know what this means right?" asked Tommy.

"No. What does it mean?" Debby asked grinning.

"Wait, do you have a job waiting for you somewhere?" he asked curiously.

"No," Debby said plainly. "I was just going to shop around in different firms until I found one."

"Well, you do now. I'm going to open up my own law firm and since your score is so high, you're coming with me," Tommy said excitedly.

"What are yo talking about?" Debby asked still happy about her accomplishment. She heard what he said, but she needed to make sure it registered right. "Calm down a second. Talk to me."

"I'm going to open my own law firm. I want you there with me. You worked hard as hell and made enough sacrifices for a lifetime. I want you either on my team or helping me. I would love for you to be my personal secretary. You'd get top pay with me."

"You never told me about this."

"I didn't have to," he said stating a fact. "I wasn't one hundred percent sure either one of us would pass. God willing, we both made it, so we going to get this real money. You with me?"

"I'm with you, and I appreciate you," Debby said, then pulled him into a huge bear hug. "We did it! We really passed the bar exam on the first try with high-ranking scores."

"I'm going to open up shop here in Atlanta. I already have a great location. It's an empty building on Gerald Street. It has four floors, and all the space necessary to build on."

"That's the busiest street in Georgia. How did you find space there?"

"A spot just opened up. I took the number down and called about the space again this morning. I sent a Western Union to the owner, and he accepted it as a down payment. Now, I'll take what's left of the money, and put it towards the firm." Seeing her eyes well up with tears stopped Tommy from talking about his plans. "What's wrong? Why are you crying?"

"I really did it, and I did it on my first try. Do you understand how hard that test is?" she said sniffing. "Now, I have a possible future. This is the best moment of my life."

They both started smiling at each other.

Chapter 14

"Debbie! Can you see my vision?" Tommy asked, staring deep into her eyes. He needed to know for sure that he was on the right path.

"Yes!" Debby said happily. She could visualize the powers that be making it all work out for the better.

"Do you like the location?" Tommy asked wondering if this was really where he needed his firm to be. In his mind it was perfect.

"I told you the location is perfect," Debby reassured him. This was the heart of Atlanta. There was no better location than this.

"What do you think about the building?" Tommy needed to know the truth. He couldn't afford a simple-minded yes man answer to his question.

"It looks like it has potential," Debby said. She continued to look around. She walked over to one of the open windows and looked down.

"Potential for success or potential for disaster?"

"Total success."

"Great! What do you think about that lobby section I showed you? Do you think two lobbies are needed?" Tommy had been trying to figure that dilemma out for several days now.

"The lobby is good. All you need is one. That area could be the receptionist area. In the other section. Put lots of comfortable cushion chairs out there. A couple of tables, flower pots, and other decorations to make it look good," Debby said adding in her women's insight.

"Where do you think I should have my office?"

"You mean, our office," Debby corrected him.

"You know what I mean," Tommy said smiling.

"You should have it on the top floor. You should make the top floor for your partners also. You will need some partners," Debby answered calmly. She noticed he was taken aback.

The word partners killed his spirit. "Like hell I do! I'm going to be the sole owner of this firm. I won't make the huge mistake I watched other men make. No open shares, no partners, no greedy foul-ups, no nothing. It's all me."

"This place needs a lot of work," Debby said nervously looking around. Nothing was completed from where she stood.

"My people are handling that. As a matter of fact, you can look around and check out the other floors. I have a call I need to make," Tommy said dismissing her.

"If you say so. You're the boss," Debby said, turning to walk away.

Tommy waited until she was gone, and grabbed his phone. He called the head honcho who was overseeing the construction operations.

"Hey Charles, it's me, Tommy."

"Hey, what can I do for you fella?" Charles asked with a raspy voice.

"I wanted to know what is your set date to be done with my law firm?" Tommy asked, removing a notepad and pen out of his shirt pocket to take notes.

"Project law firm," Charles said into the phone. He's an elderly man who's running the top construction workers in Atlanta and earned himself a powerful reputation. "That's set for nine months."

"Can your people move any faster?" Tommy asked calmly. Tommy knew more money was going to be needed.

"You know how this game works," Charles said seriously. "You're not new to this."

"I do," Tommy said while trying to figure out a set price to make the workers move faster.

"Money talks," Charles told him truthfully.

Tommy thought about the remaining money left over for this project. Funds were running low. He had already leaned into the funds Debby was pushing for security purposes while she was working. His credit was great, he knew he could get a loan, and pay it back before the year was out.

"What number you got in mind?"

"You slide me a couple thousand, and I'll chop the scheduled time down three months. That will make a six-month project," said Charles.

Tommy pulled out his wallet, and inside there was six grand.

"You said a couple of grand, correct?"

"That's correct," Charles mumbled trying to rethink a number.

"Two thousand for your pocket, and another two thousand to get things moving," said Tommy sealing the deal.

"No problem, boss. I'll put the word out and I'll give my guys a mandatory end date. No exceptions," Charles confirmed, grabbing a rag to wipe the drops of sweat from his brow.

"Where are you?" Tommy asked. He could hear a lot of noise in the background.

"I'm on the job sight," Charles answered.

"I didn't see you," Tommy replied thinking about all the crew he scanned over.

"I'm here and so is Dave. I just took a quick coffee break," Charles passed the phone to Dave.

"Hey, boss! Its Dave. What's up?" Dave asked sarcastically. He'd heard the whole conversation and knew he wasn't getting a single penny of that extra money.

"What's going on with the pipe laying?" Tommy asked.

"I'm just about done."

"Great. I'm coming down there right now," Tommy said while grabbing his hard hat.

Tommy went down to the work site, located Charles, and passed him an envelope containing the extra money. While walking away he noticed the pipe structure. Dave was telling the truth; the foundation was complete. Without the pipe laying, no one could work. Tommy was pleased with his mission. Six months was record time. The good thing is they didn't have to start from scratch. If everything needed to be stretched out from the ground up it would have taken at least a year to get this far. So, for that much he was glad.

*****

One Year Later...

The firm was finally up and rolling. Debby stood beside Tommy on the sideline, observing the wonder of all their hard work. They looked at all the people who would soon be working at their firm. It was a struggle, but Tommy finally made his dreams come true. Once he was up and fully running, Atlanta's biggest drug lord got pinched. A Mexican woman stacked with huge breasts, and an enormous backside walked through the front door of his law firm speaking Spanish. She walked over to the receptionist who responded in Spanish and was assigned to a lawyer who would thoroughly review her case.

The receptionist tapped into Tommy's line and urged him to come downstairs immediately to speak with the Mexican woman. The receptionist warned him that she was the mother of the Mexican King Pin who's been on television for the last week. Once the receptionist announced his name, Tommy's heart pounded. He rushed downstairs, instead of waiting for the elevator. He didn't want the Mexican woman to go anywhere. When he made it to the lobby area his eyes zeroed in on the Mexican woman as he walked up to her.

"Do you speak English?" Tommy asked her.

"Yes, I do," Ms. Jiminez replied. "I have money. I need my son home. Here's all the money." She grabbed her black tote bag and turned it upside down. Stacks of money dropped out all over the floor.

Tommy's eyes widened as he dropped down to gather up all the money.

"Ms. Jiminez, please don't do that. Let me pick this money up. Follow me to my office so we can speak alone."

After all the money was placed back inside the tote bag, he grabbed her arm and led the way to the elevator.

Tommy's mind was racing. There was no way in the world he was going to turn this case over to anyone else. He thought about all the hundreds he'd just seen. Once they were in his office. He sat the bag down on the floor beside his desk.

"Would you like something to drink?" Tommy asked Ms. Jiminez.

"Yes. Water please," she said in clear English.

"Debby!" Tommy called out on the phone's intercom.

"Yes sir," Debby's reply came through the speaker.

"Can you bring me a glass of ice water for our new client," Tommy asked.

"Sure, right away," Debby replied.

"Here's your water," Debby quickly returned and passed the glass of water to the lady who was crying none stop.

Ms. Jiminez took the water, and took a couple of sips. "Can you help my son? If you need more money, I have plenty. I will pay anything to get my son home. He's not a tough guy. He can't live in prison. Please, tell me a price to make it all go away. Everybody has a price," she pleaded.

"First, we need to know what happened?"

"The police knocked down my front door. There were lots of lights and dogs everywhere. Guys with big guns and helicopters were flying above. They said my boy is involved in human trafficking of immigrants. This is not true. He saves people. He gives hopeless people new meaning in life. The men with the guns said he was a drug kingpin. He ain't none of that," she explained.

"Alright, what is your son's name? Please spell it out for me. I have to go check the system to see what his charges are," Tommy asked Ms. Jiminez.

Tommy and Debby listened intently as Ms. Jiminez explained everything she knew about her son's situation. He thought about all the money that was on the floor and kept glancing at the tote bag. This was the come-up he needed. He advised her to go home and relax. He told her that he'll take the case and that the money she had in the tote bag will be enough to handle his court fees.

Once he calmed the lady down. He got her to leave calmly. He took all the information that he needed and gave her his phone number, email address, and office hours to reach him at all times. Once she was gone, he went straight to the money bag and counted the money three times. Ms. Jiminez brought him a quarter-million dollars to take the case.

Chapter 15

"I don't know you," Alfredo said, walking up to the conference door.

"My name is Tommy White," he said in a professional tone.

Tommy looked at the guard. He knew this man was nothing to mess with.

"I said, I don't know you!" Alfredo yelled in his Spanish tenor sending chills down Tommy's spine.

"Right, we don't know each other," Tommy replied, watching the man step completely inside the room.

"What are you here for?" Alfredo shouted. Stepping inside and taking a seat, he crossed his hands in front of him and cocked his head sideways examining his new lawyer.

"Ms. Joan Jiminez sent me," Tommy divulged, looking at some notes. He looked up at Alfredo to see if that name rang a bell.

"My mother?" Alfredo smiled. "Now, I know her, but you, I don't know," he said, using a scare tactic to see where Tommy's heart was. He didn't need a coward representing him.

"Your mother paid me to handle your case," Tommy informed him respectfully, looking Alfredo in the eyes.

"Why didn't you just say that?" Alfredo said innocently. His entire demeanor changed. He didn't look like a killer anymore.

"I didn't get a chance to," Tommy said, thinking Alfredo was a serious nut case.

"What's going on with my case?" Alfredo questioned, with desperate eyes, awaiting good news.

"I'm not quite sure yet. I just got your case," Tommy stated plainly.

"Don't bullshit me!" Alfredo raised his voice.

"I'm not."

"I have a no-bullshit policy. I give ya the same energy you give me," Alfredo said with a nasty Spanish accent that was semi-hard to understand.

"I can respect that," Tommy replied respectfully, doing his best to keep his client calm.

"Fly straight with me," Alfredo warned calmly. Alfredo looked Tommy up and down. He noticed that the suit he wore was outdated and run down.

"Brutal honesty is what you're going to get," Tommy said calmly. Tommy was ready to swim with the sharks. He knew this wasn't going to be a simple meeting of the minds.

"What are my charges?" Alfredo asked, not sure of what he plead not guilty to at arraignment court yesterday afternoon.

"Human trafficking," Tommy directly stated without any emotions. In his mind, he thought that Alfredo looked like a Mexican pimp.

"I don't traffic no humans," Alfredo lied.

"That's what we have to prove," Tommy told him straight, watching the guard behind the door peek in.

"What's up with a bail?" Alfredo asked, knowing damn well the federal courts are not giving no Mexican pimp a bail. It would be a cold in hell before that happened.

"I can see about a bail," Tommy mumbled, with not an ounce of confidence. The government wanted Alfredo so that meant he was going to stay right where he was.

"Don't see about it. Get it," Alfredo ordered. trying to intimidate Tommy with a little bit of pressure.

"It's not that easy. We'll have to request a bail hearing," Tommy said while jotting down notes."

"Do it," Alfredo continued with his little pressure game, which didn't affect Tommy whatsoever.

"First thing first," Tommy said, trying to sort through his case file. He was all disconcerted. He needed Debby to get with the program.

"What's your whole name," Tommy looked at a bunch of *'known as'* names. The name ran all the way down the sheet of paper.

"Alfredo Jose' Jiminez." Alfredo smiled knowing he wouldn't get away with an alias this time.

"What's your nationality?" Tommy asked because there was no check mark next to Mexican.

"I'm Mexican," Alfredo announced proudly while lifting his head with respect.

"Were you born in the United States?" Tommy knew the answer to this because of the Green card.

"Hell no!" Alfredo angrily stated.

"I hate the United States, but I love America," he said smirking, knowing full well what he just said made no sense.

"Do you have a green card?" Tommy asked, looking through some papers. There was an indication that a green card was issued to him last year.

"I have a green card." Alfredo glanced around the visiting room. He didn't like sitting in the booth area. It created a sense that he was boxed in, and he hated being boxed in.

"Skip the bullshit. What can you tell me? Remember, if you bullshit me, I'll bullshit you back," Tommy told him flat out.

"This here is a no-bullshit zone," Alfredo said while using his hands gesturing that the area they were in was a total bullshit-free zone.

"I need you to be straightforward with me. I need to know everything, so there are no surprises. If you bullshit me, you leave me blind, and it's you who will suffer. I will fight your case, but you can't string me along," Tommy said closing the file.

"You want total honesty from me?" Alfredo asked looking Tommy dead in the eyes. When he noticed Tommy didn't fold to the intimating stare he knew that he had himself a real tough ass lawyer. "I'll keep it real with you. But I promise you, if anything I say to you gets back to the prosecutor, I'll kill you and that little bitch whore, Debby." Alfredo's Mexican voice had vanished. He'd spoken in clear English.

Tommy was taken aback. He couldn't believe that Alfredo knew about Debby. He couldn't believe how proper Alfredo's English was. Here he was thinking he was dealing with a simple Mexican immigrant that got lucky. At that moment, he knew not to bullshit Alfredo Jiminez.

"Don't think I don't know about Lil' Woo and the infamous Ryder. I know all about you. I know you scored pretty damn high on that bar exam. We all pay attention to bar exam scores," Alfredo said with bloodshot eyes.

"So, you know that these scare tactics are useless and unnecessary? You know that I will fight my ass off to win your case," Tommy said while looking Alfredo in the eyes. Tommy wasn't intimidated at all. He was amazed at how much he knew in such short notice.

"I know. I just like to feel people out. This is your first case, and it's a big one. When you leave, there will be a lot of media outside. Keep your head down low, and give no responses," Alfredo warned.

"How do you know that?"

"I know a lot," said Alfredo. "Just like I know you're not going to win the bail hearing, but you are going to win my trial."

"So, you're not looking to cop-out?" Tommy asked, hoping a quick open and shut case would do everybody's nerves some justice. "So, what can you tell me about this situation?"

"I can tell you they got me red-handed. I can tell you my girls won't rat me out. I can tell you none of my girls are strays, runaways, under age, prisoners, or being forced to do things," Alfredo stated honestly.

"What about this hotel?"' Tommy asked looking at a document that explains the daily activities that transpire in his place.

"It's a whore house." Alfredo shrugged his shoulders and said it without a hint of emotion.

"I see here you were arraigned and indicted on the same day."

"Something like that," Alfredo said.

"Are you aware that all thirty-seven people who were arrested with you are all out of prison? Are you sure no one will cooperate with the cops against you?"

"I'm aware. I made that call. Also, I'm one hundred and ten percent sure no one will tell on me," Alfredo said while winking his right eye.

"So, you want no deals. You're sure about going to trial?" Tommy asked curiously.

"Fuck the prosecutor. He can ram all of them deals up his loose ass. Trial it is. No cop-outs. We don't cop-out to nothing. It's go hard or go home. I'm riding this wave all the way through," he announced using his Spanish voice.

"Are you interested in a speedy trial?" Tommy asked.

"Will you have time to prepare?" Alfredo asked skeptically.

"I can be ready a whole lot quicker than the prosecutor. Shit, he got two years or more to sort through potential witnesses, review statements, set up a game plan, run down all his resources, and force people to overwork. This won't be a simple open and shut case. Especially, since you're not going to break for no one," Tommy said urgently. He leaned in very close to the glass. He needed Alfredo to understand everything he said.

"Then push for the speedy trial. This way I can speed my way back home. Do you have enough money?"

Alfredo knew that a quarter million wasn't enough. Tommy was going to need a lot of hired help. Even private investigators cost a pretty penny to do their job correctly.

"For a trial, I will need more," Tommy said.

"If you mean to get my freedom you will need more. I don't like half-ass lawyers. I need confidence on my side. Nothing but the best. I'll send you more money."

The security guard who was watching and listening the entire time knocked on the door. He was signaling Alfredo that his visit time was up. The administration gave him a legal visit on the day all visits were supposed to be closed. And because of this, the media was all out front.

"Here's my card. It has all my information on it. It's so you can contact me at any time. If I don't answer, leave a message," Tommy explained

"When am I going to see you again?" Alfredo asked calmly.

"Anytime you want. Just hit me up, but don't abuse it," Tommy announced.

"Abuse what?"

"My kindness."

"No problem. You can keep your card. I know how and where to reach you." Alfredo pushed the card back through the small slot.

"I'll see you later," Alfredo said, before rising to leave and disappearing on the other side of the door with the guard.

Tommy gathered his belongings and was escorted to the main entrance. When he got there, he observed the full-scale media. Cars, trucks, vans, and helicopters were all waiting for Tommy. He tucked his head low and stormed out the front door.

Chapter 16

"So, when are you going to buy yourself a car?" Debby asked as she adjusted her glasses in the rear-view mirror.

"I don't know," Tommy answered, wondering where her line of questioning was coming from all of a sudden.

"You need one," Debby said honestly.

"Are you tired of driving me around?"

"Pretty much."

"Why? I thought you liked spending time with me?" Tommy said teasing her.

"I'm always with you," Debby admitted seriously.

"So, what's the problem?" Tommy asked, staring at her from the side.

"You don't pay me enough."

"So, you want me to pay you for chauffeuring me around?"

"That would be cool, but it would be much better to drive yourself."

"I'm starting to think you don't love me no more."

"Anyway, how do you feel about the case?" Debby asked changing the tempo of the conversation, hoping he went along with it.

"I can't call it."

He tried not to think about the case all the time. He knew if he was meant to win, then he would win.

"It's a tough one, ain't it?"

She was glad to be a part of his team. Winning this case would be good publicity for their firm.

"Tell me about it."

"You know them jurors are some stone-cold cookies. Some of them are unreadable," Debby said seriously. "I paid them close attention."

"I know, I saw them," Tommy said rubbing his temples.

"What I don't understand is how someone gets charged with human trafficking, but you can't find one single person to testify to this." Normally, it would be a flood gate of witnesses ready to testify, but not in this situation.

"I spoke with a couple of these women."

"What did you get out of it?" asked Tommy.

"They were grown women living their lives," said Debby, amazed.

"Not one of them had a single complaint against Alfredo?"

Debby shook her head. "Nope. Some were ready to go to war for him."

Tommy had also seen the same protectiveness in one of the older women. "I saw her grabbing knives ready to stick into someone for Jiminez."

"That's crazy," Debby said shaking her head. Her eyes were focused on the traffic. "One woman said she's been with him since she was eighteen."

"That's the blond head who just turned thirty-two last week," Tommy said remembering how crazy the woman was. All she wanted to know was when Alfredo was getting out of prison.

"Did you see any underage girls?" asked Debby.

"Nope."

"No complaints?" she asked again in curiosity.

"None."

She sighed loudly. "I don't see how the government even built this case."

"No wire tapes. No informants. No nothing," said Tommy.

"Definitely not your everyday drug prostitution ring," Debby shot back. She'd seen some real prostitution shit in her times, but this was above all.

"Certainly not." Tommy checked his watch. "You might want to hurry it up a bit."

"I got this," Debby said smirking.

"I can't afford to be late today. This is day four of the trial. It could be all over today, and I don't need the judge looking at me funny," Tommy said seriously.

"That old goat could eat a cow's dick," said Debby.

"I feel the same way. Unfortunately, we can't afford to express our true inner thoughts. That'll get us held in contempt," Tommy pointed out. "We don't need that."

"That would look very bad on our record. Especially, if we don't win," she said meaningfully.

"Make the right coming up," Tommy snapped.

"I know damn it," Debby snapped back. "That's the old goat right there," she said as she pulled up near the courthouse.

"Where?" Tommy asked.

"Right there." She pointed to the left.

"Yeah, that's him," Tommy said studying the man.

"I should run his ass over," Debby mumbled under her breath.

"I will not handle your murder trial."

"Why not?" Debby asked while quickly slowing down.

"Because he's a judge." Tommy shrugged.

"So what?" Debby said. "He's not fucking superman. He ain't invincible."

"You can't just run over a judge and expect absolutely nothing to happen."

"Lighten up a bit. I was only joking," she said cutting her eyes at him.

"My mind can't comprehend no more jokes. It's game time, woman."

"Put on your game face then," Debby said.

"I always got my game face on partner."

"Definitely," she said showing support.

"And that's how it's supposed to be," said Tommy getting his mind ready for another day in court.

"Hey look, there goes that bitch ass prosecutor and his bitch ass buddy. Damn, that's three birds I can kill with one stone. This car being the stone and them three jackasses being the birds," said Debby narrowing her eyes.

"Stop talking crazy."

"No problem, sir," Debby said sarcastically while still thinking about running the government's team over dead. She laughed at the thought.

She drove the car into the employee and officers of the court parking section. She kept an eye on the judge and prosecutors who were now talking in front of the entrance door. She swerved her car into a parking space not too far from where the group of men was conversing.

A few minutes later, the duo team was heading toward the courtroom where the trial was being held. When they stepped inside, they both looked to the right where the prisoners and inmates sat. Alfredo was sitting there smirking at them. They saw him try to wave, but the retainers stopped him.

Tommy let Debby walk over to the bail lift and the court arm officer. She ordered them to remove the prisoner's upper restraints and allow him to readjust his clothing. Once done she joined Tommy at the defense table. They didn't have much time to prepare before the court's guard announced everyone to rise for the appearance of the honorable judge Matt Limber. The court was officially in session.

The court reporter announced the case by number. "Case 12341," she yelled loudly so everyone could hear her. "Case of United States verses Alfredo Jose Jiminez for trial." Once she finished, she quickly looked around the courtroom before taking her seat.

"Would counsel please state their appearances for the record beginning with the government," said the judge.

"Prat Herber and Douglas Groom for the United States. Good morning, your honor," said Prat.

"Good morning, your honor. Tommy White and Debby Wilde for the defense."

"Good morning. Mr. White," Judge Limbar said politely. "I take it we're going to continue with the trail for Mr. Jiminez."

"That is correct your honor. The government wishes to call its final witness," said Prat.

The questioning of witnesses lasted all day. They took a break at lunchtime, but resumed once lunch was over. None of the government's witnesses moved the jurors. However, the defense questioning left a deep impression on all the juror's minds.

Mr. Jiminez took the stand and held up pretty well. His story was a whole lot more believable than the government's. On direct and redirect, he held his ground firmly. By the end of the day, the people were sent home thinking about the case. They weren't allowed to discuss the case with the outside world, especially not the media.

Tommy and Debby rode back to the office together. Not much was said, however, both of their minds were racing. Everything was on the people now. Twelve jurors stood between a man and his freedom.

"Quick thought," said Tommy.

"What's that?" asked Debby.

"I'm buying a car tomorrow."

She smiled.

Chapter 17

Traffic around the courtroom was exceedingly heavy. As Tommy got closer to the courthouse, they saw people holding signs, banisters, and Mexican flags. These were Mexican people here today to show their support for the Mexican drug lord accused of pimping women. He pulled his car into the parking lot and drove up towards the front section. The first parking space he saw, he quickly pulled in. When he looked to the left, he saw the prosecutor pulling in four spaces down from him. He wondered if he was going to pull some sort of trick to win the case. He knew that victory was going to be his as long as the prosecution team played fair. Tommy turned his head avoiding the prosecutor's stare. He grabbed his suitcase, snatched the keys from the ignition, and opened his car door.

Tommy strolled directly to the court entrance and walked through the section preserved for court officers. After checking in, he walked over to one of the court booths to request to see Alfredo before the trial began. Walking towards the elevator he saw the rest of the prosecution team. They didn't look as confident as they did when the trial first started. They crowded inside the elevator. When they saw Tommy, they respectfully nodded their heads while the elevator doors closed.

After arriving at his floor, he quickly stepped off the elevator, allowing someone else to stand in his spot. Tommy strolled down toward the main section where the lawyers from both sides wait. Once inside, he checked to see if his request went through. The clerk announced that Alfredo will be in the conference room after the prisoners were counted and cleared.

An hour later, he waited for Alfredo to arrive in the holding cells. Tommy walked up to the cell doors and told Alfredo that he was going to pull him out right away. He walked off and searched for the guards. He told the first guard who his client was, and got confirmation that the request went through.

Tommy sat down, placed the suitcase on the table, and pulled out a document. He scanned through the premade trial transcripts and had to retract some of the witness' statements. This trial was a circus. Everyone swore to tell the truth, yet everybody was lying.

Tommy ran through his notes, and reread the letter sent to him from his client. He laid everything out before him. The little room he was in was painted tan and brown. It was small and tight-fitted. Before him, there was a fiber glass window with the bottom section wide open. The space was big enough to reach his hand through. He sat on a small stool that was the same as the one for prisoners. There was a camera on the other side looking directly at the meeting section. Tommy glanced upwards at it. He knew it was for his protection, but the fiber glass window was more than enough.

An officer accompanied by a Marshall walked to the door and opened it.

"I'm federal Marshall Hall. We will be escorting your client down to this room shortly.

"Why are you here?" Tommy asked curiously.

"Because if he blows trial, we don't know what the crowd of people might do."

"What do you mean?" Tommy asked frowning his face.

"I mean, it's possible that your client might have some dangerous immigrants out there waiting to cause problems," Hall said seriously.

"What kind of problems?" Tommy asked.

"Possible riots," Hall replied.

"Are you serious?" Tommy asked in disbelief, looking at the huge dark-skinned man with closed eyes and a round face.

"Your client is not only a pimp, he's a drug warlord. Today, the trial is set to be finished. Now, depending on the jurors, you know the deliberation stage. Which could take forever. We believe violence could break out," Hall said.

"This is all unproven allegations," said Tommy.

"That's the stance you going to pull?" Hall said frowning.

"There's no stance," Tommy answered. He knew that if these allegations came up in court, it will look bad for his client.

"Sir, it is."

Tommy stared at him hard. "No. Really, it's not.

Hall sensed his anger. "Hey, we're on the same side."

"Sure, you're right," Tommy said sounding phony. "When are you going to get him?"

"Momentarily," Hall said checking his watch.

"That's great," said Tommy, then turned his head back to his papers.

Tommy was aware that the Marshall was just standing there staring at him. He did everything in his power not to look up at the guy. He heard the door close, and when he looked up the Marshall was gone. Five minutes later, he heard chains and voices. He knew that the officers were moving a prisoner.

Looking upward, he saw a prisoner walking by. It was Alfredo. He noticed they escorted him to a booth close by. Tommy rose up and tapped on the window. No one acknowledged him. After a few seconds, the Marshal appeared and stood in front of the door. Tommy watched the Marshal signal that they took Alfredo to the wrong conference room.

Alfredo was standing in front of the doorway facing Tommy. He nodded his head in acknowledgment. Once the Marshal opened the door, he led Alfredo to his seat. Alfredo wore an all-black suit and tie. His shoes looked very expensive, and his face was shaped up smoothly. He looked very professional and innocent, but that was a joke. He was the complete opposite.

Marshal Hall opened the door again and stepped outside. He stood there looking at the back of Alfredo's head. He was very familiar with the drug lords' case and situation. He'd been in pursuit of Alfredo for years. This is why he chose to take a personal interest in his case. He wanted to see Alfredo behind bars for his criminal operations.

The Marshal was aware of the potential dangers Alfredo and his crime team possessed. It would be easy to sit in a crowd creating confusion, or triggering a riot. They could easily make things seem racial. Alfredo had more than enough power and money to have all the people outside under his control. He knew this, but no one else seem to be aware of the serious threat Alfredo posed to this courthouse. Hall knew if the verdict came back guilty, there would be an uproar, and he wanted to be there to stop it.

Alfredo looked over his shoulder and saw out the corner of his eye that the Marshal was behind him right outside the door. He faced Tommy and smirked.

"Hi, Tommy."

"Hello, Alfredo."

"How are you?" Alfredo asked sounding sincere.

"I'm fine," said Tommy as he shuffled through his papers.

"That's good," Alfredo said moving his hands to loosen the cuffs by sliding them off the bone around the side of his wrist.

Tommy looked up making eye contact. "What about you?"

Alfredo gave him a half-smile. "I'm a mess."

"I can only imagine," said Tommy. "This trial is rough."

"I try to relax my mind, but the stress is overbearing," Alfredo said leaning back.

"Do you believe in God?" Tommy asked.

"Of course, I do," Alfredo admitted.

"Do you pray?" asked Tommy.

"All the time. Why do you ask?"

"Praying helps," said Tommy.

Alfredo smiled thinking of his mother. "I've been told that all my life."

"Well, try doing it."

Alfredo's smile widened. "You sound like a priest, instead of a lawyer about to win the biggest case in his life."

"I'm just trying to show my concern," said Tommy, placing the papers down in front of him.

Alfredo nodded. "And it is noted."

"I pulled you out to give you the breakdown of what's going to be happening next."

"How much time do we have in here?" Alfredo asked.

"About ten minutes," Tommy said.

Alfredo folded his hands in front of him. "What do you think about how's it's going so far?"

"You can never tell with these kinds of cases," Tommy said honestly.

"What do you think about the jurors?" Alfredo asked.

"They're really hard to read."

"I noticed that too," Alfredo said.

"I have noticed that jurors two and ten don't like the prosecution team."

"I noticed that too," Alfredo said leaning forward, resting his forearms on the table. "I wasn't going to say nothing, but I see how they twitch and turn when they feel something isn't right with the prosecution's story."

"Today is going to be the day I get to speak to them. I'll be providing the court with my closing statements," Tommy informed Alfredo.

"Did you hear how everyone keeps lying?"

Tommy nodded his head in agreement. "Honestly, that lying is clear to the jurors, and those lies are killing the prosecutor's case. I don't want to give you any false hope, but if these jurors do their job, today could be a beautiful day for you."

"It will also give you your first big win," said Alfredo.

"I'm going to make something happen today," Tommy said while pushing some papers towards Alfredo. "Read this and when you're done, I'll see you in court."

Six hours later, the courtroom was silent while the defendant delivered his heartfelt story. He drove his high points directly into the juror's minds. They all listened intently. He held their gaze while he spoke, and they clung to each word. When Tommy elaborated on his story, there was no doubt the jurors were captivated. They were intrigued by his speech. They nodded their heads when he touched on key points. Some of them whispered to each other. Although their facial expressions did portray their true feelings, no one truly knows what they will decide.

A female juror was assigned to announce the finding.

"Today, we the jurors have reached our decision, and we find the defendant Alfredo Jiminez, not guilty of all charges," she announced, then returned to her seat.

Everyone who came to support Alfredo began to celebrate his win. His mother ran to his side and embraced him tightly.

"Thank you so much, attorney White. Thank you for helping me and my son," she said with tearful eyes.

Chapter 18

A telegram came to Tommy when he left his office. Since his big victory with the Jiminez case, his name became well known. The new *Shark Lawyer* in town is what he was called. He seized the telegram from a young man who was Mexican. The man bowed his head respectfully and walked off. Tommy opened the telegram and his eyes widened in surprise. Alfredo sent Tommy an invite to an event he was hosting at his mansion in Mexico called The Black-Tie Gala. Alfredo also sent Tommy a round-trip plane ticket. It was great timing because he didn't have any meetings scheduled or court cases.

When he returned to his home, there was a package on his front step. Curiously, he picked it up and shook it, but didn't hear anything moving inside. He brought the box up to his ear and didn't hear anything ticking. Grabbing his car keys out of his pocket, he carried the unknown box inside his house.

Once inside his house, he quickly tore open the package that revealed two cards, and six stacks of money bands that fell to the floor. Tommy stared at the money for a moment, then decided to open up the cards one by one. Inside were the thank you notes from Alfredo and his family, and another invitation to Alfredo's event.

Tommy was happy. He knew that defending Alfredo would be very beneficial, and now he'd get to see firsthand how much. If he hadn't made up his mind to go before, he was definitely going to that Black Tie Gala event now.

Feeling excited, he went through his suits and found the best black suit in his closet, and paired it with a black tie and black shoes. He was going to be a white man looking like the Black Stallion. He tossed everything on his bed and started packing his bag. *I was born for this lifestyle*, Tommy thought smiling.

A few days later, he checked in with Delta Airlines and boarded his flight without any hiccups. Before boarding the plane, he contacted Alfredo letting him know that he was on his way out to Texas. Tommy packed a three-day bag with extra garments just in case. He sat in the coach section and vowed to never do this again. He kept looking at the address on the invitation card. The place was in Waco, Texas. A place he'd never been before.

As the plane soared through the sky, several flight attendants pointed him out as the lawyer who won the big case. Tommy turned his attention to the clouds, and he looked over the city. The world was a beautiful place. The Jiminez case put Tommy in a powerful spot as a lawyer and he was just getting started. His phone line was blowing up with criminals who all wanted to obtain him as counsel. However, he didn't have the time for small-time cases. The real deal is where the money was, and that's what Tommy was about. This was another reason he was on a flight going somewhere he'd never been before. He had a feeling The Black-Tie Gala would be worth his while.

Several hours later, he arrived in Texas at the Lionel Prime Air Port. This was one place he'd never thought of traveling to. When he walked through the tunnel in the airport, he made a short detour to the bathroom, and then to the baggage claim to retrieve his luggage. Once he stepped outside, he observed a small crew of female Mexicans. One of them was holding a sign with his full name on it. This was Alfredo's welcoming committee for Tommy. He looked at all the women and wondered which one he would be fucking before the night was over. He waved at them and flashed his identification card. Two of the women walked over to him and escorted him to the awaiting white limo.

All the women climbed in the limo after Tommy and immediately started comforting him by rubbing his body. The limo driver wasted no time cutting through the traffic while the women inquired about Tommy's flight. On the outskirts of the city, there was a lot of farm land and beautiful houses. The scenery was completely different than what Tommy was used to. He didn't see too many tall high risen buildings like the city holds. There were palm trees, trains in the street, and a lot of weird shaped two-story houses. Everywhere he looked was peaceful, even though he knew it wasn't. Tommy knew that these peaceful looking streets harbored some of the most violent gangs in the United States.

After a twenty-five-minute drive, they drove for three minutes on sandy grounds before coming to a forest green landscape. Then the most beautiful scene he'd ever witnessed came into view. It was a sight straight out of the bible. A mansion structured like a king's palace appeared. Exotic trees and animals came into sight. Some of the girls who spoke clear English announced that they had arrived at Alfredo's sanctuary. Tommy noticed an alarming number of vehicles near the palace. He knew those were the other guest who was invited. Something told him it would be a marvelous event.

"Do you like it?" the young girl Mary asked clinging to his arm.

"It's incredible," Tommy replied.

"I'm pleased that do," Mary smiled.

"Is this all Alfredo's?"

"Yes," said Mary smiling.

"How long did it take to build such a place?" Tommy asked in awe.

"Rumors have it that it's been around since the days of Moses. Of course, they did plenty of upgrades," she said continuing to make small talk.

"Do you live here too?" Tommy asked curiously.

"We all do," Mary confirmed.

"How many bedrooms does it have?"

"There are thirty bedrooms," Mary's smile widened.

"Damn! That's a lot." Tommy was expecting something like ten to twelve. So, to have close to triple that amount blew his mind.

"That's nothing. His other homes have more than that," Mary offered still smiling.

"Are you for real?" Tommy asked.

"Absolutely." Mary nodded her head, showcasing her pearly white teeth that shined bright with her glowing butter milk complexion. She was just as pretty as the other girls, but the way she glowed made her stand out.

"Damn, it seems like he got it all."

"Pretty much," Mary shrugged.

"Are all those cars his too?" Tommy asked because he wasn't so sure now that he'd seen how wealthy Alfredo was.

"No, those are the early guess," she said, looking in the same direction he was looking in. "His fleet of cars are inside the garage."

"How many guests are here?"

"What's expected?" Mary sought confirmation.

"Yes," Tommy replied.

"Close to a thousand."

Tommy's eyes widened. "Damn! Is there a ballroom?"

"Yes. It's very big. It can hold up to two thousand people. That's the legal capacity. Very spacious," she assured him.

Tommy couldn't believe what type of person he was dealing with. Thinking of the names people refer to him by really made sense now. There was one name that had stuck out to him was, *'The Hand'*. They referred to him as a drug warlord, not a kingpin, as he was used to hearing. *A warlord.* That's huge now that he thought about it. His name never was mentioned in the hall of fame for drug dealers. Most of the names there are dead men. He's a living drug lord. And now this drug lord has befriended him.

Looking around, he saw the balloons, streamers, and cards on display that read, *'Welcome Home Alfredo'*. He also noticed the entourage of females awaiting his arrival. Through the crowd, Alfredo emerged smiling. The man looked like a million bucks. Stepping out of the car, Tommy smiled at his client and newfound friend.

"Alfredo!" Tommy acknowledged.

"Tommy boy!" Alfredo greeted him back with open arms.

"I'm glad you made it. How was your trip?"

"It was great," said Tommy. "Is all this yours?" he asked sounding more excited than he intended to.

"It's all mine and my family," Alfredo said patting Tommy on the shoulder.

"Thanks to you it will remain mine. It's because of you I have my freedom," Alfredo said, opening his arms. "They would have taken everything from me if you would have lost. It wouldn't have just been a prosecution, it would have been an execution. But, thanks to my guest of honor, that didn't happen."

"Guess of honor?" Tommy cut in surprised.

"That's right. This gala is for you," Alfredo smiled.

"Really?"

"Sure, my friend," said Alfredo grinning. "I want to introduce you to my world. If not for you, I would probably be dead. People like me can't do the jail thing. Prison is beyond my comprehension. I could never survive at my age. No, I have to die free while possibly swimming in some hoochie-coochie." Alfredo shared a quick laugh with Tommy.

"Thank you, Alfredo. Let me get my suitcase."

"Nonsense. You will do nothing in my presence except relax and have some fun," Alfredo said seriously. "Now, come on inside," Alfredo invited.

Tommy was bubbling with anticipation. "Lead the way."

He watched Alfredo turn around while two beautiful women grabbed each arm. Tommy wasn't surprised when two women seized his arms as well and escorted him.

"Follow me," Alfredo said, walking through his front doors. "This is my lovely home. We call it the main palace. To the right is the free room which is an open space filled with entertainment for the young ones," Alfredo announced.

For approximately two hours, Tommy was led around the entire premises. Every square foot of the property. He was blown away when he was led through a man-made cave leading to a man-made waterfall. Tommy was shown exotic exhibits of a million dollars' worth of paintings, drawings, and architecture by the time they were done viewing the property. He then was taken to his room where his belongings awaited him. Everything he needed to prepare for the Black-Tie Gala and the rest of his stay with Alfredo, was provided. He didn't even need to pack a bag.

Once Tommy was done getting dressed, he went to exit his room and was met by another entourage of women to escort him to the gala hall.

"Are you here for me?" he asked.

"We're here to escort you to the ballroom," the ladies answered simultaneously. One of them looked like Mary.

"Mary?" Tommy asked.

"No. I'm India, her twin sister," she said with a mischievous smile.

"There's two of you?" Tommy asked a rhetorical question with bug eyes. He shook his head smiling. "Let's go, then."

The moment the gala doors opened; Tommy was blown away. Everything was amazing. The sight was something words couldn't explain. The place lit up, and it seemed as if he'd stepped into a different world.

"Ladies and gentlemen, the man who set me free just walked in. Please give him a round of applause for Tommy White," Alfredo announced at the entrance for his newfound friend.

The entire place exploded with applause. Over a thousand people broke their necks trying to see Tommy. Doctors, lawyers, senators, mayors, gangsters, judges, music artists, porn stars, police officers, correctional officers, other drug lords, a few Mexican Cartel members, Russian Cartel members, and other leaders of crime families, all turned in his direction. Tommy acknowledged them all.

When things calmed down, Alfredo made special time for him. He introduced him again to a few good men who wanted to retain his services. By the end of the gala, Tommy had over two dozen new clients. They all left their names, numbers, and large retainer payments to seal the deal. Tommy didn't know it, but his entire world was destined to change. Before he left to go back home, he received a total of six million dollars in retainers because he was able to bring the warlord home.

Chapter 19

It didn't take long for Tommy to get familiar with Mr. Myers's case. It was the same ole, typical sex trafficking charge. The only weird thing about the case was the hearsay. The federal agents had a mountain of paperwork on Mr. Myers. Yet, not one solid piece of evidence. For days, he studied the case inside out. In the federal system, prisoners run an extremely high risk of being convicted on hearsay. The federal system even has a charge for drug offenders who have no drugs called, *Ghost Dope*. Normally, things boil down to how bad the government wants you.

Tommy sat in his office looking out the window at Debby. She was living up to his high standards, and she hired some pretty interesting people. However, he was wondering about a paralegal. He needed one to help prepare the case. He rose from behind his desk and opened the door.

"Debby!" Tommy called from his office. "Are you busy?"

"Whenever I'm in the office," she straightened out her blouse. "I'm always busy, but not too busy for the boss. What can I do for you?" she smiled.

"Did you check into a paralegal?" Tommy asked, adjusting himself on the chair's cushion.

"Actually, I did," she answered with eagerness. "Marlene Hiss. Hold on, I'll be right back."

Debby rushed away to retrieve some forms that looked like applications, then rushed back inside the room, and handed Tommy Marlene Hiss' online application.

"This is her credentials, and there's a small photo of her on the second page," Debby explained.

"This is great work," Tommy said, continuing to read the papers. "When does she start?"

"I have her coming in on Monday."

"Did you finish with the notes from the Myers case?" Tommy needed to know.

"Be right back," Debby stormed out of Tommy's office again. Rushing to her desk, she pushed aside some folders until she found what she was looking for, then ran back across the hall. "These are the notes, suggestions, and all the key points. We have to be in the courtroom in one hour."

"Hearsay?" Tommy read the first word in the notes.

"Absolutely!" she nodded her head.

"I must've missed something," Tommy frowned.

"Everyone missed something," Debby smiled, knowing she was the only one who observed that the prosecutor's case was based on hearsay. Nothing solid at all.

"Where's Mr. Myers?" Tommy asked.

"He sent a text stating that he was on his way down to the courthouse," Debby replied. "The other attorneys sent text messages also. Everyone is on their way to the courtroom. We need to get going as well."

"I'm glad I have you on my team," Tommy said while reviewing the notes.

"What's that about?"

"I noticed that the elements of the charges haven't been proven to any degree. It's like the prosecution is handing us the case," Tommy admitted. "You know what? Let's get going." Tommy gathered all his court papers and placed them in his suitcase.

They walked side by side down to the courthouse. They both thought about how in sex trafficking cases, there are usually other members involved. Tommy's client has a single case, but he's being charged with 18 U.S.C 1591(b), which is one count of conspiracy. The alleged victims who identified him have never seen him, spoken to him, or even been in his presence. The Crawford law forbids hearsay as evidence.

Once they arrived at the courthouse, they saw their client, waved, and kept walking through the employee's side door to the courthouse. Tommy was confident in knowing he could shut the case in triumph. He was ready to get started.

After clearing the security detector, they strolled down to the courtroom labeled trial case MR10112. Shortly after they arrived, Mr. Myers and his entourage strolled down the hallway greeting his newly recruited lawyer. Not long after he arrived his original team approached the doors. People began entering the courtroom once the doors were open.

Quickly after the room filled up, the judge entered the room from his chambers. Tommy watched the prosecution team enter the room in a haste. They were all discombobulated and unorganized. He noticed Mr. Myers sit directly behind him until he waved him up front. They were now sitting right beside each other. The court reporter stepped up holding a sheet of paper.

"Case number MR10118, United States v. Mr. Myers. This case is on for trial. This is week two. Counsel, please state your appearances for the record beginning with the government."

"Dominque Makes and Erica Sidney for the United States. Good morning, your Honor."

"Good morning, Mr. Makes and Ms. Sidney," the judge responded.

"Good morning, Judge. Tiffany Scott, Hines Pitch, and Tommy White for Mr. Myers."

"Good morning, Ms. Scoot, Mr. Pitch, and Mr. White. And good morning to you Mr. Myers."

"Good morning," Mr. Myers said, through clenched teeth. He couldn't stand the sight of all these court officers. Yet, he kept his composure, knowing all this nonsense would soon be over.

"Today we will be starting day thirteen on the trial for Mr. Myers. We'll hear testimony from the government witness. Direct and cross-examination will be done. We will now start the trial. The government may call its star witness."

"Thank you, Judge. The People of the United States would like to call Ms. Anita Souls to the stand."

Everyone watched while a fragile, fair-skinned woman in her early twenties sashayed towards the front section of the court. Her long legs looked skinny and sexy with her crimson color dress on. Myers didn't recognize her. In fact, he didn't believe he'd ever seen her before in his life.

"Who the hell is she?" Myers asked Tommy and the rest of his team of lawyers.

"She's the star witness," Mr. Ptiche whispered, adjusting his tie on his neck. His creepy beady eyes fell upon the witness.

"She doesn't look confident about taking the stand. She's shaking like a leaf," Myers said in a whisper.

"She's definitely nervous," Tommy agreed, keeping a close eye on the witness.

The moment Anita repeated her oath, she began to tell her story. Most of what she said was all hearsay. She testified in a third-party manner, and not as someone with direct information. Tommy was already on top of the situation.

"I object, Your Honor," Tommy stood up with his hand extended slightly upward.

"Why are you objecting?" Judge Taples asked, looking at the entire defense team. His eyes settled on Tommy.

"I wish to raise the Crawford law. This law forbids the introduction of testimonial hearsay as evidence."

"Well, it seems we have to give the jury some instruction towards the Crawford Law which hinders the prosecution case, being that Anita is the star witness. Hearsay testimonies are forbidden."

"I object," the prosecutor blurted.

"Objection noted," Judge Taples said calmly.

The quick thinking on Tommy's behalf saved the defense case. The other lawyer in the courtroom didn't catch on at first. They were glued to Anita's words until Tommy saved the day. Because of this, he was allowed to make a strong case with his closing argument. He'd already formatted the perfect closing speech.

Tommy decided to close out by pointing out all the legal holes in his client's case and driving a nail into them. He rose from his chair and looked at his client who held a smirk on his face. Everyone sensed that the case was already beat, but still, the final blow had to be drawn.

"Ladies and gentlemen of the jury. We're here today to seek justice in a sex trafficking case. The government must prove, inter alia, that the defendant, Mr. Myers recruited, enticed, harbored, transported, provided, obtained, advertised, maintain, patronized, and solicited each of the victims while knowingly, or recklessly disregarding measures of force, fraud, coercion, or any combination of such to cause victims to engage in commercial sex acts. This is what the title 18 U.S.C section 1591(a) entails. A key element of such a charge is driven by the first word, showing conspiracy and sex trafficking. Here my client is the only person indicted on this charge. However, to conspire, it must be two or more individuals. The government did not show any proof of this crime."

"The National Center for Missing People discovered a suspicious advertisement featuring a woman who appeared to be an underage girl. This advertisement was on backpage.com. Backpage.com is for facilitating prostitution."

"Through hearsay, the FBI began collecting my client's hotel, Facebook, and email records. Nothing connected my client to any criminal activities. I challenge the validity of the search warrant for the admission of evidence seized thereafter. The government did not show that there were five or more persons who were accused of a position of organized sex trafficking, a supervisor position, a position of management, or continued criminal activity resourcing income. Without these key elements, the jury must find my client innocent of the charges and must acquit." Tommy walked back to the table giving up his time.

Chapter 20

"How's the recruiting going?" Tommy asked Debby as she walked into the front section of the building.

"I can't call it yet," Debby responded, looking through her files.

"Why not?" Tommy wondered why she didn't have a solid answer to a question so simple.

"Because I haven't interviewed anyone yet," Debby said, thinking about all the potential applications she received. She was still weeding them out.

"Are there any potentials?"

"Actually, I'm glad you asked that," Debby announced smiling at the first two applications and resumes she'd pulled.

"Why?" Tommy asked wanting to hear more.

"Because I have a young shark coming in today," Debby smirked innocently. "She's hardcore on all levels."

"At what time?" asked Tommy.

"At ten o'clock."

"Who is she?" Tommy asked trying to think about all the upcoming, hard-hitting attorneys.

"She's a highly recommended lawyer," Debby said confidently giving the lady high praises.

"Recommended by who?" Tommy asked as the lines on his forehead stretched out into a frown.

"Billy Harvey," Debby said proudly knowing that everybody whose somebody knew him.

"What?" Tommy was amazed at the recommendation from such a high figure in the game of law.

"That's right, I got the email last week."

"Why didn't you tell me?" asked Tommy.

"I had to hear from the lady herself first. And I needed to make sure this was really what she wanted," Debby said smiling. She knew he was excited by her news.

Tommy leaned back in his chair. "So, have you spoken to her?"

Debby nodded. "Yup, that's why she's coming in today."

"Anyone he recommends please hire immediately, and make sure she's on our team," said Tommy eagerly.

"There's' a slight problem," said Debby, her smile quickly disappearing. "She doesn't want to work for us. She wants to work with us," Debby explained.

"What?" Tommy frowned.

"She wants her own section in the building. Billy advised me that she needs her own firm, and to be her own boss," stated Debby, waiting for Tommy's reaction.

"Damn! She's demanding a whole section? Well, give it to her. She can run the west wing. She'll answer to no one. Did you check her out?" Tommy asked. He had been trying to figure out who was going to run that wing and hiring her would answer that question.

"I ran a thorough background check on what I could find without her social security number. She's a real shark. She was mostly an add-on to the majority of cases I found, but she ended up taking over each case. And, get this," Debby said quickly. "You'll never guess this one," Debby said amazed.

"What?"

"She never loses."

"What? How many cases has she had? Are they state or federal?" Tommy asked not believing what Debby just said about the young lady due to show up soon.

"I have that answer for you. Hold on," Debby looked through some files. "Here we go. She has both. In the state, she has twenty-one wins, no losses. In the federal system, she has two wins, no losses."

"So, she's done federal law and won?"

"That's the way it looks," said Debby. "She won one at a trial, and the other was won on appeal."

"Does she do criminal and civil cases?" asked Tommy eager to learn everything he could about her.

"Yes."

"She sounds like she deserves the west wing. How long has she been in law?" Tommy asked eager to make a final decision.

"Two years," Debby said, remembering what she'd read in the file.

"Wow! I thought you were going to say more than that. That's wonderful for two years. Sounds like she has a great future ahead of her."

Debby looked at the notes she held in her hand. "We also got some other potential lawyers, but she's the most promising," she said looking at the names of the other applicants.

"Make sure she joins our team. Accommodate her on her wishes. We need sharks in this firm," Tommy said while looking around the office, and visualizing people working hard for the betterment of his firm.

"No problem. Only the best," Debby said smiling knowing she'd made Tommy happy with the news she'd given him.

"There's someone at the door. I think that's your new girl. Wow, she's fifteen minutes early. That speaks volumes,"

Tommy said while looking at a beautiful young lady strolling towards the front desk.

"Hello, my name is Brooklyn Brown. I'm here for my ten o'clock interview. I was told to ask for a Ms. Debby Wilde."

"Hello ma'am, this is Ms. Wilde right here," Tommy said and walked away smirking. Tommy couldn't believe how beautiful Brooklyn was.

"Hi, I'm Ms. Wilde. Can you have a seat and I will be right with you in just a moment. You're fifteen minutes early, that's a great impression," Debby complimented.

"Better to be early than to be late," Brooklyn replied with confidence.

"That's correct. Being late shows all kinds of laziness. It's an impression you never want to leave on anyone."

"Tell me about it," Brooklyn agreed.

Once Debby called Brooklyn back to her office, they concluded their interview on a good note. Debby offered her the position on the spot. As soon as Brooklyn accepted, she advised her that she could start immediately on the west wing.

Chapter 21

"For my first case, I want to take on Ezra Gommez," Brooklyn said looking through the firm's case files, and landing on that name.

"Why would you want such a high-profile case?" Debby asked looking at Brooklyn like she was out of her mind for suggesting such a thing.

"Because I know I can win," Brooklyn said confidently while holding Ezra's files in her hand.

"Are you certain?" Debby asked, knowing that Ezra was a serious client.

"I'm positive," Brooklyn confirmed with a smirk.

"Well, if you are confident that you can win this case, I'll allow you to take it, but Tommy will be in the courtroom."

"That's not a problem," Brooklyn agreed.

"Are you sure?" Debby asked taken aback.

"I'm sure. He'll get a chance to see how I handle cases upfront," Brooklyn said knowing that's what he would probably want anyway.

"Well, that case is up for a hearing today," Debby said looking at the dates corresponding with cases.

"Give me everything you got on it," Brooklyn ordered aggressively, ready to get to work and make magic happen immediately.

"The case won't be called until after lunch. Is that going to be enough time for you?" Debby asked.

"More than enough," Brooklyn said while she waited for the files. She knew his case was dealing with drugs. She'd caught wind that he was accused of smuggling one hundred kilograms into the United States twice a month.

When Brooklyn got the file, she rushed to her office and closed the door. She scanned through all the paperwork and checked for mistakes and violations. She knew there was going to be many. While scanning the files, she got a text from Tommy. He greeted and welcomed her to take over the Ezra case. He advised her that he'll be in the courtroom throughout the proceeding, but she'll be the one handling the case.

By the time lunch came and went, she was already down in the courtroom. She patiently waited for the doors to open. While waiting, she somewhat introduced herself as his new lawyer. Tommy just happened to appear while the introductions were going on. He confirmed that she'll be handling his case while he played on the passenger side. Once the bailiff opened the doors, Brooklyn and Tommy sat together, and Ezra sat directly behind them. They watched the judge walk in, as everyone rose briefly for him.

"Case number KS-00855, The United States versus Ezra Gommez," The female officer of the court announced. She handed a stack of folders to the Judge Skeptically.

"Will the parties please state their appearance for the court record starting with the prosecution, and then the defense," Judge Skeptic announced with authority.

"America's United States Attorney Doug Loom, and Pat Miths for the government," Doug said proudly.

"Brooklyn Brown led defense lawyer, and Tommy White for the defense of Ezra Gommez."

Judge Skeptic's booming voice spoke again. "We're here today for the arraignment as to Ezra Gommez. The defense has waived the public reading, and how does the defendant plead?"

Without looking back at Ezra for his plea, Brooklyn stood straight up and spoke clearly. "Your Honor, my client, the defendant pleads not guilty."

"All right, let the record reflect that I have entered a plea of not guilty to the indictment against Ezra Gommez. The matter will be assigned to me. The speedy trial time is excluded from today until the first pretrial conference. Not to extend beyond the ninth day of May," said Judge Skeptic.

"Your Honor, I have here a motion for a dismissal of the indictment. May I please approach?" Brooklyn asked respectfully, Glancing at Tommy who was shocked. She winked at him.

"Yes, you may approach the podium," Judge Skeptic replied respectfully. "And the prosecution may approach as well."

Tommy looked at Ezra who was standing right next to him. "She knows what she's doing," Tommy assured.

"You must be a mind reader because that's exactly what I wanted to know," Ezra asked somewhat concerned.

"Why aren't you up there?"

"Do you want to get this case thrown out?" Tommy asked suspiciously.

"Of course, I do my boy," Ezra said with a peaceful smirk stretching across his face.

"Then let her work her magic. She knows what she's doing. Her record streak of wins is amazing. Trust me, she got you," Tommy said to Ezra.

"I thought you were going to be handling the case," Ezra said.

"I am handling the case. You see me here, don't you?" Tommy asked respectfully.

"Okay, I'll let you guys get me free."

"What's the dismissal for?" Judge Skeptic asked Brooklyn while leaning forward.

"Your honor, this court has repeatedly ignored defective indictments," Brooklyn spoke respectfully.

"How so? Please excuse such accusations against the court," Judge Skeptic asked not liking the argument Brooklyn brought forth right off the jump.

"Your honor, this document I have is the proper format for which an indictment must be filed. A quick review of our law will show this indictment against Mr. Gommez is in fact defective and must be dismissed," Brooklyn said in a respectful whisper so that the court wouldn't take offense to her argument.

"Your honor, there is nothing defective about the indictment. It was properly filed," Doug said, knowing he was lying through his yellow teeth. He knew he'd been getting away with defective indictments for decades. He also knew that he really couldn't afford to challenge her argument. If so, it would have a waterfall effect, and hundreds if not thousands of inmates would start flooding the court with the same argument.

"Just a minute. Let me review the formats," Judge Skeptic said taking the documents from Brooklyn. Moments later he glanced up with a frown. "I do believe Ms. Brooklyn has some merit to her claim," he said as he glanced back down at the papers and quickly read over the papers. He observed that there was no seal, no correct elaboration on the charges, and worse of all, there was no official signed signature of the Judge or prosecutor. That in itself was a violation.

"You two may have a seat," Judge Skeptic told both counselors.

Judge Skeptic waited until they were seated before he picked up his pen and began jotting down notes.

Doug leaned in close to Brooklyn as she stepped behind the table to sit.

You're the first person in decades to challenge an indictment counselor. I hope you understand what type of flood gate you could be opening." Doug was agitated and embarrassed.

"I'm here to shake things up. Justice will be served correctly while I'm around," Brooklyn said ruthlessly before sitting at the defense table.

"Hey what's going on? What did you just do?" Ezra asked.

"I'm getting your case thrown out," Brooklyn said over her shoulders.

Judge Skeptic put his pen down and everyone got quiet. "I, Judge Skeptic announces, that in the case of the United States of America against Ezra Gommez, and in light of justice, and after full consideration of a defective indictment, I announced that the case is dismissed with prejudice."

Everyone in the courtroom went crazy. Brooklyn looked at Ezra with distaste, and nodded as she packed up her suitcase. She then met up with Tommy at the door and left. Four days after Brooklyn beat the big drug lord's case, she received an invitation that was addressed to her. However, when she opened it, she saw that it wasn't for her after all. She rushed over to the main section of the building to forward the invitation to Tommy.

"Hey, I received something in the mail that had something addressed to you on the inside," Brooklyn said, walking into the main section of the law office.

"Who sent it? What's the name on the return section?" Tommy frowned.

"Ezra's name is all over the envelope," Brooklyn announced skeptically. She had an idea of what this was about.

"Wow! He's inviting me to his estate," Tommy said while reading the invitation and looking at Brooklyn.

"I don't think you should go," Brooklyn said, seriously concerned. She was aware that Ezra was nothing to play with.

"Why not?" Tommy asked, clutching the invitation in his hand.

"Because he's not a normal person. His invitation will come with strings attached and most likely a threat of some sort." Brooklyn said this as a fact, not an opinion.

"I have to go," Tommy said and walked away.

When the time came around, Tommy had a black suit on ready to shoot out to Ezra's home to attend the Black-Tie Gala. Once there he was introduced to hundreds of drug lords, King Pins, congressmen, and women. Dozens of people gave him money for retainers. His night was going well until Ezra pulled him to the side telling him he had a gift for Tommy that was in the trunk of his car. When the night was over, Tommy checked his trunk and found 100 Kilograms of crystal white powder. The note on top of the kilograms said; *Thanks for beating the case. This will start you off right, I insist.*

Tommy's heart pounded on his way to his house. He was so paranoid of getting pulled over with the bricks of coke. He made sure to do the speed limit and respect all the street lights and signs. By the time he made it home, it was nine o'clock at night. He took the duffle bag out of his trunk and went inside. He went straight to his room and dropped the duffle bag on his bed. *What the fuck am I gonna do with all this?*

The chiming of his phone shook him from his thoughts. Grabbing his phone off the bed, he realized he'd got a text from Debbie.

Debbie: Billy Harvey, the lawyer who recommended Brooklyn, wants to invite you to his home where he's throwing a small get-together with other lawyers.

Tommy was surprised that such a heavy hitter in the defense world wanted him at his home.

Tommy: When is the party?

Debbie: The party is going on right now.

She then sent him the address.

He contemplated if he wanted to go or not because he didn't want to leave so much work at his house. He decided that going to Bill Harvey's home would be a great way to put himself in with the big league. After putting all the coke in his closet, he grabbed his keys and headed out the door.

Chapter 22

Tommy finally arrived in the nice section of Bankhead. When he stepped out, he looked at the mini-mansion and walked towards the front door. He rang the lion-shaped doorbell and heard the doorbell from the inside. A middle-aged white woman with huge breasts and a lot of Botox in her face answered the door.

"May I help you?" she asked.

"I'm here to see Mr. Harvey. I was invited. My name is, Tommy White."

"Oh, yes! Come in!" she said stepping to the side so Tommy could walk in. "My husband's been waiting for you."

Tommy walked in and followed her to the living room where he got the surprise of his life. In the living room, there were about 10 other men, and a bunch of half-naked women walking around drinking and snorting cocaine.

"Hey, Bill! Tommy White's here!" his wife called to a tall Tom Cruise looking man.

Billy Harvey was standing by a bar and walked over to Tommy and his wife.

"Hey, Tommy. It's finally nice to meet you," he said reaching his hand out for a shake.

Tommy took his hand and shook it. He looked around the room still shocked by what was happening. "Umm, it's nice to meet you too, Mr. Harvey," Tommy replied. "So, what's with the invite?"

Billy walked over to the couch in the middle of the room and gestured for Tommy to have a seat. "Please call me,

Bill. I invited you here to welcome you to the big leagues," he said, grabbing a glass full of scotch off the table in front of them.

"After that win you got for Ezra and 'The Hand' case, it definitely took you up."

"I appreciate it. I didn't think my status would rise that quickly," Tommy said feeling great about himself.

"It sure did," Bill said, reaching over to the table to grab a mirror with thin white lines evenly spaced out. He grabbed a straw and took a sniff. "You want some?"

"No, thank you," Tommy said, surprised that a well-known lawyer was sniffing coke. "Are we even allowed to do that?"

"Tommy boy! We are big dogs now. We can do what the fuck we want. As long as we keep winning and earning big bucks," Bill said taking another sniff. "Argh! This trash ass coke. Shit doesn't even do anything!"

Tommy started to think, and his mind went to the coke Ezra had placed in his trunk. He had an idea, but he would have to ask Bill.

"Do all the big lawyers sniff cocaine?"

"Ha! Lawyers, judges, prosecutors, even the damn attorney general likes to sniff some once and a while."

That's all Tommy had to hear for his street mind to start working. He figured he could sell the coke he had to Bill, and he could introduce him to the other heavy hitters in the law world. He just had to play his cards right.

"Bill, what if I told you I could get you some way better quality coke?"

"I'd tell you to go ahead and bring it!" Bill said anxiously. "This coke I've been getting is getting worse and worse. Can't keep wasting my money on this. How much?"

Tommy had to do the math in his head. He remembered when he was young, Lil' Woo told him that a brick of coke could range from $25,000 to $35,000, depending on the quality. He figured that since he got the coke from Ezra, it must've been good. He thought if he could sell every ounce for $1,200, he could make $43,200 off each brick. That's $4.3 million tax-free.

"About $1,200 an ounce," Tommy told him.

"Really?! That's a lot cheaper than what I get them for! I want 4 ounces!" he said anxiously.

After discussing the plans of when Tommy would get it, they agreed to meet the next day at Tommy's law firm. When Bill arrived, Debbie was surprised to see him.

"May I help you, Mr. Harvey?" Debbie asked.

"Yes, I'm here to see Tommy. He should be expecting me."

After Debbie beeped Tommy's desk and got the okay, she told him he could go on up. When Bill arrived at Tommy's office, he tried some of the coke and instantly felt his face numb. Being satisfied, Bill gave Tommy an envelope with $5,000 and told him that he will definitely be in touch with him.

When he left the office, Tommy sat back in his chair. He couldn't believe he'd just sold drugs to a well-respected lawyer in Georgia. He never imagined breaking the law again. Not since he was young. His mind began to wander and his thoughts fell on Ryder and Lil' Woo, wondering what they were up to.

Chapter 23

Harlem, New York…

"This has to go down," T. Mills said aggressively.

"I know! We need to get this dude Lil' Woo, as soon as possible," Joe Black agreed.

"Do you think he'll buy the weight off of us?" T. Mills asked doubtfully.

"Probably, if he needs it." Joe Black shrugged knowing if Lil' Woo was desperate for work, the chances of him taking it would be higher.

"The word on the street is he's looking for a hookup," T. Mills reminded.

"Well, the agents gave us enough to make the setup. We can charge a small fee to make sure he'll cop the weight from us," Joe Black suggested, knowing they'd have to come correct.

"When do you have to meet back up with the agent?"

"He just text me an hour ago and told me he'd be around here at six-thirty. So, I guess in another hour or so," Joe Black said while looking at his new internet connector watch that cost him a rack.

"What time did Lil' Woo say he would reach out to you?" T. Mills asked, hoping like hell they had enough time to deliver without being caught up.

"He said after he handled some personal business, he'd hit me up. He pushed the time 'til around eight tonight," Joe Black said while setting a vibrating alarm to two different times to remind him of the meetings.

"That gives us plenty of time to set up. You got your microphone and camera in your belt buckle ready?" T. Mills asked while checking all his surveillance devices to make sure they were working.

"I'm always strapped up and ready," Joe Black said, pointing to each digital gadget showing everything was prearranged and ready for recording. It took him a while, but he'd gotten used to being a cooperating witness. All they had to do was catch a major player, then their case would disappear.

*****

Lil' Woo cleared the metal detector for the second time. He hated when the searching correctional staff made him clear the detector more than once. He never brought anything into the jail that could be considered contraband. Besides, even if he wanted to, his pops wouldn't allow it. It was strange when out of nowhere one of the cops decided to strike up a conversation while he waited in the visiting section.

"Damn, you're the second visitor today who came to see the old man. You must be his son. You come through for him quite often, that's a good thing. I hardly see other cats getting visits from their kids," the correctional officer stated.

"Man, forget all that. Why every time I come here you always make me go through that metal detector twice? It's like you trying to make a brother get cancer from the radiation," Lil' Woo asked, completely aggravated with the whole process.

"Nah, lil' man, its protocol," the correctional officer lied.

"Protocol for me only, huh?" Lil' Woo asked, shaking his head.

"You be looking suspicious, dude." The officer scratched his head, knowing he didn't have to do all he did when Lil'

Woo came to see his dad. "Everything is suspect and is subject to scrutiny. It's nothing personal. If you feel that way, you can write a complaint," the correction officer teased.

"Do I look like I would write a damn complaint? Shoot, there are plenty of other ways to handle oppression," Lil' Woo said, eying the man with a deadly stare.

"Is that some form of threat?" The officer tensed up and adjusted his posture. He didn't like what Lil' Woo said, and he wasn't trained to take threats lightly.

"You must think I'm boo-boo the fool. I ain't threaten you in no shape, form, or fashion. Could you please leave me alone, and let me get my visit? There ain't no reason for you to even be talking to me. I ain't here to be harassed by a correctional officer. I'm here to see my pops," Lil' Woo said, unwilling to fall into the trap the officer was obviously trying to lead him into.

"You got that young man. Enjoy your visit," the officer said, walking away feeling defeated. He stood at a distance watching Lil' Woo until his visit showed up.

"Hey pops! What's up?" Lil' Woo greeted walking towards the table his pops was just escorted to.

"My main man! Come give your pops a hug," The Plug said, giving his son a handshake, and fatherly hug.

"All right pops, you squeezing the life out of me," Lil Woo said, struggling to get loose.

"Man, I love coming down here to see something different. I'm so tired of being around men all day. Look at all these beautiful women down here. I'm glad you came to check on me," The Plug said honestly.

"I'm glad I made you happy. You need the birds-eye view to see as many women as you can. These girls here are wack as hell! I'm going to send you some real pictures this week. I'll have one of my little jump offs come see you soon, but I really can't stay too long." Lil' Woo looked at his watch, knowing he needed to get to it and go.

"Why not?" The Plug asked him, wondering why it sounded like he was in a hurry.

"I got to meet up with some dudes so I can get right," Lil Woo informed him.

"Who do you deal with?" The Plug asked with raising concern. He didn't want his son in the game, but his son was grown.

"Right now, I'm trying to get something from two dudes; T. Mills, and his boy Joe Black."

"What!? Them two fools are still out there nickel and diming?" The Plug asked, visibly pissed.

"What's up? Why up flipping pops? They've been around for decades getting money."

"Be careful man," he said glancing around.

"Why? You know something I don't know?" Lil' Woo asked feeling uneasy.

"Them two fools are the same idiots who helped them federal agents set me up," The Plug said in a low voice so no one around could hear.

They continued their visit until Lil' Woo had to go. Lil' Woo thought about his father's words long and hard when he left the prison. His pop told him they weren't on his paperwork, but his lawyer told him they weren't his friends, and couldn't be trusted. Lil' Woo changed his plans to meet them immediately.

*****

At eight forty-five, the two men came to realize Lil' Woo wasn't coming. They repeatedly dialed his number to no avail. On the eighth time, they finally gave up hope. The last time they called Lil' Woo's number it was no longer in service. When Agent Lee was notified, he was mad as hell to find out Lil' Woo didn't take the bait.

136

Chapter 24

Two Years Later…

"What's with all the people?" Laura, a woman who Tommy just met, asked.

"I don't know? Looks like someone famous just pulled up," Tommy replied. He was enjoying a late-night drink at a hot spot restraint in the downtown area of Atlanta when a whole bunch of people began swarming the entrance.

Ever since Tommy began serving Bill Harvey, his reputation and status quickly rose and he made a lot of good connections in the law world. Even though he wasn't trying to be a full-time drug dealer, he still served other lawyers, judges, and politicians to keep him in his good graces.

"Well, they must be famous because the owner just came out to greet them," Laura said.

The moment Tommy saw who walked through the entrance, his heart dropped. He couldn't believe his eyes and he thought his mind was playing tricks on him. Lil' Woo walked past the owner who greeted him with Ryder wrapped around his arm. He kept his eyes on them the whole time they went to their table. Once he built the courage to confront them, he got up and approached their table leaving Laura by herself.

"Excuse me," Tommy said when he finally reached Lil' Woo and Ryder's table.

"My name is Tommy White. I don't know if you remember me, but—"

Before Tommy could finish his sentence, Ryder jumped out of her seat and screamed in joy.

"OH MY GOD, TOMMY!" Ryder said, excitedly. She gave him a big hug and then turned to face Lil' Woo. "Woo, remember Tommy? From the old hood?" Before Lil' Woo could reply, Ryder turned to face Tommy again. "Where have you been? What are you doing here?" she asked excitedly.

"What am I doing here? What are you doing out here?" Tommy asked.

"I live out here now! We just moved down here for Woo's music career. He just did a show. Now, answer my question!"

"I live out here," Tommy said while looking Ryder in the eyes. "I have my own firm. I'm a lawyer."

Tommy couldn't believe how happy Ryder was to see him, even though Lil' Woo seemed like he couldn't remember him. He didn't care. As long as Ryder remembered him, that was all he wanted. Tommy thought he could never forgive Ryder for breaking his heart, but the moment he saw her, that went out the window.

"So, what are you doing now?" Tommy asked Ryder, hoping she wasn't still stuck in her old ways.

"Not what I used to be doing," she said proudly. "I manage Woo and promote his music and shows now."

"That's great!" Tommy replied, but in his mind, he wanted Ryder to be back in his life so he offered her a deal. "But, how about this? You come and get a job at my firm as a paralegal while trying to get your law degree like you wanted to when we were young."

"Are you serious? Woo! What do you think about that?" Ryder asked Lil' Woo.

The whole time Tommy and Ryder were talking Lil' Woo just sat back and listened. He remembered exactly who Tommy was and even heard of him beating big cases. He just felt bad for abandoning him when they were young and didn't know what to say.

"That's cool with me. I need a couple of lawyers now that I'm about to get into the industry," Lil' Woo said calmly.

"Great!" Ryder replied.

The trio talked for a couple of hours before they decided to part ways. When they made it outside, Lil' Woo asked Ryder if she could get the car.

"Sure," she replied.

"Bye Tommy. I can't wait to see you next week at your firm." Rider gave him a big hug and kiss on the cheek before leaving.

"I'm sorry, Tommy," Lil' Woo said, once Ryder was gone.

"Sorry for what?" Tommy was surprised. He didn't know what Lil' Woo was talking about.

"For leaving you when we were young," Lil' Woo said, looking Tommy in the eyes. "Me and Ryder decided it was best for you to leave New York and pursue your dreams. If we came along, we wouldn't have done nothing but hold you back."

Tommy didn't know what to say. The whole time he left New York he thought that the people he considered family abandoned him, but in actuality, they let him go to better himself. He now understood why they never came, and couldn't be mad at Lil' Woo.

"You know, the whole time I thought you guys didn't give a fuck about me. Now I know y'all just did what was best for me, and I appreciate it," Tommy said then gave Lil' Woo a brotherly hug.

"I told you before, once you're my homie, your like family. And I don't forget about family."

Chapter 25

The next day, Tommy walked into his office and was rushed by Debbie.

"Tommy, where have you been? You're late," Debbie said anxiously.

"I overslept. I ran into some old friends last night and stayed up too late. What's going on?"

"Mr. Ezra's been calling all morning. He told me to tell you he needs to speak with you immediately."

"Okay? I'll call him soon as I get to my office."

Tommy wondered why Ezra was so pressed to talk to him. Since that night he gave Tommy the bricks of coke, he'd been buying the drugs off him to sell. He made sure not to let anyone know about his dealings. Especially, not Debbie and Brooklyn.

Once he made it to his office, he went directly into his drawer and pulled out his burner phone to call Ezra.

"Tommy!" he heard once the phone stopped ringing.

"Ezra. What's going on? Debbie said you've called all morning?"

"Meet me at the spot in an hour," Ezra said, then hung the phone up.

Tommy looked at the phone in confusion. He wondered what was so important that Ezra needed to see him now. He'd just bought a couple of bricks off him not long ago, so it couldn't be about that.

Tommy grabbed his keys off his desk and told Debbie he'd be back in a couple of hours before heading out the front door.

*****

Tommy pulled up to the small farmhouse on the outskirts of Atlanta, in Macon, GA. When he stepped out of the car, he was immediately rushed by a group of men with AK-47s.

"WOAH! What's going on? I'm here to see Ezra!" Tommy yelled.

"Hands up!" An unknown man ordered.

Tommy complied and was searched for any weapons on his person. Once cleared, the man who patted him down gave a nod to the man who told him to put his hands up. He said something to his walkie-talkie, and a couple of seconds later, Ezra came out the front door.

"Tommy, my friend. I'm sorry about this. I just need to be extra careful," Ezra said, puffing his cigar. "Please, come in."

Ezra turned around and went back inside. Tommy went up the steps to the front door and followed him. Once inside, an armed guard closed the door and stood by. Ezra sat on a couch still puffing the cigar.

"Ezra, what's going on?" Tommy asked once he was seated.

"Tommy, I have some bad news," Ezra said putting his cigar out. "I can't do business with you anymore."

Tommy was disappointed. He didn't know what he'd done wrong and wanted to know why because these types of people just don't stop dealing with you and let you live.

"It has nothing to do with you, Tommy," Ezra revealed. "It's these fucking Russians! They want to start a war over territory. It's cost me too much money, and now I must lay low."

Ezra gave a head nod to one of his men and he left the room. A few seconds later, he returned with a book bag and placed it next to Tommy.

"That's 10 uncut kilos of cocaine. That's for you to keep. I'm sorry, Tommy, but this is it between the two of us."

With that, Ezra got up and left the house with his bodyguards heavily protecting him.

*****

One Month Later…

Tommy walked into his office with his mind working a thousand miles per hour. He had to get ready for court soon, but his main concern was about a plug. He couldn't provide his normal requests for cocaine due to the low quality. He was down to his last three bricks, and that was thanks to Ezra. Tommy needed to find a new plug as soon as possible.

Just as all seemed lost, a light bulb went off in Tommy's head. He remembered Ryder telling him one night that Lil' Woo wasn't into nickel and diming anymore. He figured he could call her, and see if Lil' Woo could help him out. Tommy grabbed his phone, scrolled to the icon that said Ryder, and pressed it.

"Hello?" Ryder answered on the second ring.

"Hello? Ryder?" Tommy replied.

"Good morning, Tommy. What's up?" Tommy heard Ryder say.

"Good morning, to you too. Are you up or still in bed?" Tommy asked looking at the clock to see that it was early.

"I'm in bed still, but I can talk," Ryder replied.

"I need some help."

"What kind of help?"

"I need some shit," he said trying to talk in code.

"Tommy, I don't do that anymore. I'm trying to change my life."

"What are you talking about?" Tommy asked confused.

"You're talking about fucking for money?!" Ryder said irritated.

"Good God, no! I'm talking about some Coke," he said, saying the last word quietly. Tommy was waiting for a response, but when he didn't hear a reply, he thought Ryder hung up on him.

"Is it personal?" Ryder finally asked, hoping the answer was no.

"Hell no! I'm been moving some, but I need a new plug."

"Oh," she said relieved. "You need to call Woo and ask him. If he asks how you know, tell him I told you."

"Okay. I'm gonna call him now."

After hanging up with Ryder, Tommy called Lil' Woo immediately.

"What up?" Lil' Woo said after the first ring.

"Woo! It's Tommy, I need to talk business.

Chapter 26

After talking with Lil' Woo, Tommy was on his way to New York to pick up some bricks. Everything went smooth on the way there. When he made it to New York, he rolled his window down to smell that good Big Apple air. He drove to a parking lot on 145th street, and Riverside and parked. He pulled his phone out and called Lil' Woo to tell him he was at the spot. A few minutes later, he saw Lil' Woo pull up and park next to him. He signaled Tommy to hop in his car with him.

"What's good, Woo?" Tommy asked, giving Lil' Woo some dap when he got in the passenger seat.

"About 10 bricks, that's what's good," Lil Woo said, handing him 2 bricks with a chemical tester. "Go ahead and check it out."

After testing the bricks, Tommy was satisfied and handed Lil' Woo the money.

"I hope we can continue to do business together," Tommy stated.

"Yeah, just hit me up whenever you need more," Lil' Woo agreed.

They gave each other a handshake and Tommy stepped out. He went to his trunk and stashed the bricks in the empty spot where his spare tire usually sits. After concealing the drugs, he jumped in the driver's seat and headed back down to Atlanta.

*****

About halfway down the highway, Tommy needed to stop to get gas. He pulled off the exit and stopped at a gas station in Springfield, Virginia. He stepped out and went to the gas pump to fill his tank. When looking around, he saw a group of teenagers standing on the corner of the gas station. Tommy wasn't a square and knew that they were most likely selling drugs. After pumping his gas, he went back to his car and was on his way back to the highway. Before he made it there, he saw police sirens behind him and a blue and grey police cruiser. He pulled over to the side of the road and waited for the officer to approach.

Tommy was scared shitless. Even though he knew he had 10 bricks of cocaine in his trunk, he knew not to panic. When the officer approached his window, he rolled it down.

"May I help you, officer?"

"Seems like your brake light is out," the officer said. "Where are you coming from?"

Tommy knew the officer was lying. He knew his brake lights and headlights were fine. The second thing he noticed was the officer had on a Fairfax County badge. He heard through a friend that Fairfax County police always played dirty, and lied about their cases so they could get a conviction. Luckily, Tommy knew about their tricks and knew more about the law.

"Are you sure, officer?" Tommy asked.

The officer picked up on his attitude and got a little aggressive. "I'm gonna ask again, sir. Where did you come from?"

"I just stopped by to get some gas."

"Did you know that area is a well-known drug area?" the officer asked.

"No, I didn't. Is there a problem?" Tommy asked, knowing that some bullshit was about to occur.

"Is that weed I smell coming out of your car, sir? I'm gonna need you to step out," the officer said, then stepped back.

Tommy gave out a little chuckle and shook his head. "Wow, that's how you guys get away with an illegal search? You use the 'smells like weed' excuse?"

The officer was a little aggravated by what Tommy said to him, so he stepped forward and tried to open his door. When he couldn't open it he was pissed.

"Listen, I know you just bought some drugs back there, so you better comply with my commands, or I'm gonna have to make shit worse for you!"

"Well, just to let you know, I'm a great lawyer in Georgia, and I know the law. What you're doing completely violates my rights."

"Is that right? Well, I am the law, and I can do what the fuck I want right now. So, if I say it smells like weed coming out your car, the only two that know it doesn't is me and you, smartass," the officer said with a smirk on his face.

"Yeah, me, you, and this small little camera I have on my dashboard," Tommy said, pointing to the camera he had installed just in case situations like this occurred. "I'm sure your boss would love to see this, and the media."

When the officer noticed the camera, his demeanor changed. "Well, I might have made a mistake. Maybe I didn't smell any weed. Sorry for the inconvenience," the officer stated, then walked back to his car, and sped off.

"Fucking dick," Tommy said, then blew out a sigh of relief.

Even though he knew he shouldn't have taken a risk of talking back to the officer due to the bricks in the trunk, the lawyer side of him kicked in, and knew he wasn't about to just lay down easily. Tommy started his car up and headed towards the highway. He couldn't wait to get back home so he could get back to business.

Chapter 27

One Year Later…

"Congratulations on the Victory case, Tommy!" Lil' Woo said.

Tommy, Lil' Woo, and Ryder were at Ryder's house celebrating the win. Tommy had represented a man named Victory, a drug lord of the Atlanta City Bush Mafia, who was accused of drug trafficking and murder. After today's victory, Tommy's name was all over the news.

"Thanks guys, for throwing this little party. I wish Debbie and Brooklyn could have made it. Debbie had to stay at the firm, and Brooklyn has a case she has to study. I wish you could meet Brooklyn. She reminds me so much of you."

"So, what's the plan now?" Ryder asked putting three glasses and a bottle of Dom Perignon on the table.

Tommy grabbed the bottle and poured everyone a glass.

"I want you to work with me at the firm. You can still help Lil' Woo with his music, but you could help him more legally if you're with me."

"Just like when we were young. You always wanted Ryder close to you," Lil' Woo said, and everyone laughed.

"Seriously," Tommy said once they settled down. "Now that we're a team again, we can make some shake. With you supplying me and me supplying these squares, we could do a lot of damage."

Lil' Woo knew what Tommy said was right. If he wanted to become a full-on rapper, he would need someone who had connections like Tommy to make it happen. Tommy raised his drink in the air and made a toast.

"To making it big."

"To making it big!" Ryder and Lil' Woo said together.

Just as they made the toast, Tommy's phone started to ring. When he looked, he saw an unfamiliar number.

"Sorry, I need to take this."

"Go ahead," Lil' Woo said, taking a swig of his drink.

When Tommy stepped outside, he answered. "Hello?"

"Is this Tommy White?" the voice on the other end asked.

"Yes?"

"My name is Abu, and I'm trying to obtain your services for a friend."

Epilogue

"FREEZE! DEA!"

A swarm of agents ran into the empty warehouse where T-Mills and Joe Black set up a local drug dealer.

"FUCK!" Lil Fatz yelled, surrendering to the ground.

"FUCKIN' FEDS! FUCK YALL!" Joe Black yelled while getting handcuffed, putting on a show for Lil Fatz.

When Joe black and T. Mills were handcuffed and put in the back of the agent's car, they were driven down the street to an alley and were uncuffed.

"Great job, guys. Here's your money," the agent said handing them each a brown paper bag.

"That's what I'm talkin' bout!" T. Mills said, looking in the bag.

"So that's it for us now, right?"

"Not quite. We have one more job for ya'll," the agent in the driver's seat said.

"What? I thought we were done after this!" Joe Black yelled.

"Listen here motherfucker! I say when you guys are done or not!" the agent who handed them the money said.

"Woah calm down. It's just this last time guys. I promise," the other agent tried to defuse the situation.

"Man, a'ight. Who is it?" Joe Black asked, heated by the way the agent spoke to him.

"Lil' Woo," the agent said.

"Lil' Woo? We already tried to get him and it didn't work," T. Mills said.

"We have a new game plan. Seems like Lil' Woo moved down to Atlanta to pursue his music career. Our source says he's still selling drugs, so we're gonna send you guys down there."

T. Mills looked at Joe Black who looked like he didn't know what to do.

"So, what do you think?" T. Mills asked Joe Black.

"Fuck it. We might as well get this shit over with," he said, looking at the agents.

"When do we leave?"

TO BE CONTINUED…

Check Out Music By Ghetto The Plug

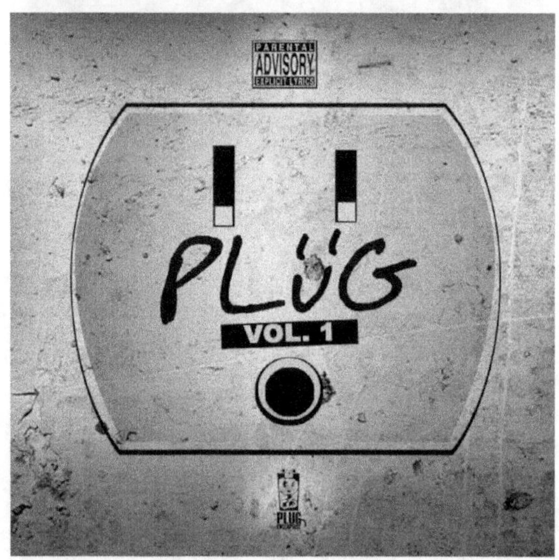

**Also search and buy my music on
https://tinyurl.com/ghettotheplug
It's worth the buy!**